The Musings of
Dessie
Twelvetrees
From school to stage

The Musings of
Dessie
Twelvetrees
From school to stage

Gary Buckner

BROWN
DOG
BOOKS

Published under licence by Brown Dog Books and
The Self-Publishing Partnership, 7 Green Park Station,
Bath BA1 1JB

www.selfpublishingpartnership.co.uk

ISBN printed book: 978-1-78545-340-3
ISBN e-book: 978-1-78545-341-0

Cover design by Andrew Prescott
Internal design by Andrew Easton

Printed and bound by CPI Group (UK) Ltd, Croydon, CR0 4YY

Foreword by
Sir Gideon Cole

I first met Dessie when we both performed in a production back in the early Seventies and it became patently obvious to both of us that we were going to become immediate pals and workmates. He at times could be a scoundrel of the highest order and sadly like a lot of scoundrels who walked a very thin line, was taken from us much sooner than he should have been. When we first met he was young, debonair and extremely talented and it was very clear to everyone who trod the boards with him that they were working with a very special actor. We appeared in an episode of *The Saint* for ITV and on completion of filming we retired to a local public house where we were introduced to a young actor called Oliver Reed. Two days later we were found in Regent's Park asleep near the lions' enclosure. I still don't know how we got there. We met again some weeks later at an audition for a new situation comedy called *Are You Being Served?* Dessie was by far the best actor there but was overlooked for someone less talented and slightly paler.

For the record, I never passed the audition either. During the late Seventies I was lucky enough to work with Dessie on a production of *A Midsummer Night's Dream*. Dessie excelled in the role of Oberon's servant Puck and he very nearly stole the show from the actor who played Oberon, and that just happened to be me. Dessie's first marriage to actress Nina Forest unfortunately ended when he was exposed by a Sunday newspaper that took great delight in destroying the marriages of people they secretly envied. Dessie was exposed by the newspaper's photographer, caught in a very large bed enjoying the company of a pair of busty twins from Finland whose entry in the Eurovision song contest evidently reached number twenty six in the hit parade in England. He then had the good fortune to be cast as Colin in the long running soap *Brandon Road*, a programme that ran for some ten years until the mid-Eighties. It was while he was touring in the ironically named *No Sex Please We're British*, that Dessie's first love, Susan came backstage to say hello.

A year later Dessie and Susan were married and they settled in Brighton where they went on to have two lovely children, Sherry and Ian. A couple of business deals in the Nineties didn't go as planned and things became a bit of a struggle, but the theatre work was still coming in as was the occasional piece of television work. As Dessie's second divorce to Susan was looming on the horizon, one particular late-night heavy drinking session brought him a stroke of luck that went some way towards providing Dessie with some sort of security for him and his two lovely ex-wives. Dessie was introduced to animator Catherine Cross who was looking for someone to voice her new animated children's character *Dapper Duck,* a cartoon series commissioned for the BBC. Dessie needed the work and reluctantly accepted the offer. *Dapper Duck* became a worldwide success and for the next ten years Dessie worked two days a week and could afford to drink champagne again in the bars and pubs on the South coast. Dessie always worked hard and at times partied even harder and unfortunately his liver finally admitted defeat, and on one cold and frosty Tuesday morning in November he took his last curtain call. Dessie Clive Twelvetrees was an actor's actor and a fine friend. I'll miss him, the laughs and paying for his double vodkas. I hope that you enjoy the first memoir of the finest actor that should have but unfortunately never got the opportunity to play James Bond, a role that was most definitely written for him

Introduction

Dad died just over a year ago and to our eternal shame he died alone. He used to say especially after a drink or two that he always wanted to die between the thighs of actress Angie Dickinson, a woman he loved but sadly never met. Dad wasn't a famous actor but he was on the television a fair bit, usually being clobbered by Roger Moore or some other star from a late Seventies or early Eighties crime show. My brother and I used to say that if we got five people into a room and we showed them a picture of dad, three would say 'I know him but don't know his name', and the other two would say 'isn't he the bloke who was in that programme last night'? The answer would be yes, but you still won't remember his name. He was for most of our lives a rubbish dad. He was always turning up late to take us out, and he was at times an even worse husband to our mum who put up with him because she always loved him just like we did.

His days away 'filming' seemed to get longer and longer. He used to turn up late with presents as big as houses as an apology for missing yet another family party or birthday. Six months ago my brother Ian rang to say that he and his wife had begun to clear out dad's flat in Chelsea. It was while they were going through some old photos and books that they made a surprising discovery.

They found some letters and it seems that dad had been asked twice by two separate publishers to write his autobiography taken from the piles of diaries that he had written throughout his acting career. This book, as hopefully you shall see, begins from the very day he left school and for us some of the details are not easy to read, but we have to admit they are sometimes entertaining and occasionally quite funny.

Dad was a young mixed-race boy growing up in the Seventies and it becomes clear that he was hopeless at trying to work in a normal job and that acting seemed his only salvation. In this book taken from his diaries, he describes his time as a male model, an aspiring actor and unfortunately soft porn star, up until the time that he became a 'feed man' for an old music hall star. He packed a lot into the first year of his career.

My brother and I are proud to say that dad had a reputation in the business as 'an actor's actor'. He was well liked and well-respected despite being a terrible scoundrel and flirt. He always used to tell anyone who would listen that one day he could be having tea with Prince Charles and the following day downing a pint with the Krays. It was total rubbish of course but coming from dad it sounded believable. So, we hope you will enjoy the first instalment of the very strange Seventies trawl through the life of:

Dessie Clive Twelvetrees, stage and screen actor, male model, comedian, ladies' man, and our lovely much missed dad.

Sherry Shaw and Ian Twelvetrees

MONDAY, JULY 15TH, 1970

I have a name, although hardly anybody at this horrible school could remember what it was. After years of torture and pain Desmond Clive Twelvetrees has finally taken his leave of Featherstone High School, and I thank God for that. I was neither clever nor stupid so therefore I became invisible to the sadistic bastards who masqueraded as teachers in that dump. About two months ago I had an appointment to meet Mr Parker, the careers teacher, to talk about my future. In between long slow drags on his Senior Service he asked me what I wanted to do once I had left school. After a second or two I answered honestly that I had always fancied having a go at being an actor. The prick started laughing and I do believe he didn't stop until he went into the staff room to tell everyone else. I am the result of a quick knee trembler between my mother Beryl and a particular randy West Indian bus conductor possibly called Ronald or possibly Donald. Mum doesn't know which. So, Desmond the half caste boy from Southall, has left school for good and is now looking forward to six weeks off before I seek work at the labour exchange.

TUESDAY, JULY 16TH

One day. One lousy day, that's all my mum has allowed me to stay in bed for. Tomorrow I have an interview at the AEC factory. They make buses at the AEC factory, and my randy dad a bus conductor. Is she having me on or what?

FRIDAY, JULY 17TH

Shit, I've got the job. I know I'm not exactly Brain of Britain but I'm going to be picking up bloody nuts and bolts off of the factory floor. Jesus, a one-eyed cat could do that. I start on Monday on the princely sum of £1 4d a week. Mum went out tonight and got drunk on port and lemon. Some horrible old bloke carried her home and dumped her on the sofa. I think he went home.

WEDNESDAY, JULY 22ND

This really is a horrible job. I'm working with a load of old women and they're all about fifty and their language is worse than mine. One old bag keeps touching my bum and saying stuff like she wants to 'break me in'. I know what she means and she's got no bloody chance. She has a passing resemblance to Winston Churchill and she smells like rotting kippers.

FRIDAY, JULY 24TH

One really good thing about this place is that they have lots of clubs and things to do. Tonight the drama club are meeting in the clubhouse so I'm going to go. Back at home now and the drama club was ok. Sheila, the woman in charge, got me to do a bit of reading from a film called *The Family Way*. She said I was good and that I had a natural ability to express myself. I told mum what Sheila had said and all she could say was 'it sounds to me that she thought you wanted to piss all the time'. It's little wonder I suffer from a lack of confidence. Sheila has enormous breasts. I shall go to sleep tonight and dream of them.

SUNDAY, JULY 26TH

It seems that I have joined the drama club at just the right time. In six weeks we are going to perform *Treasure Island* to a load of old pensioners. I have been chosen to play the part of Jim Hawkins and there's lots of lines to learn. I must stop thinking of Sheila. It could be bad for my concentration. I went to Woolworth's yesterday and bought a single by Lulu. It could be rubbish but I bought it because of her picture on the cover. Mum came home last night blind drunk again and this morning a big ugly brute called Ken was at the kitchen table. The fucker ate our last egg.

TUESDAY, JULY 28TH

I got called in to see Bill, the floor supervisor, this morning so I thought that I might be in trouble, but how can anyone not pick up nuts and bolts from the floor the right way? He said that I'm not as stupid as he thought I was and would I like an apprenticeship to train as an upholsterer. I said yes, as its got to be more challenging than picking up nuts and bolts for a pound a week. In the canteen at lunchtime I told the old bag who keeps touching my bum about the job. She said: 'That doesn't surprise me, old Bill's been having it off with your mum for years.'

WEDNESDAY, JULY 29TH

I went to the Odeon tonight with my only old school friend Tommy Smith to see *Psycho*. It was an X certificate but Smithy had a plan that would get us in without any bother. We arrived at seven and Tommy's sister who had just started her job as an usherette, had left the fire escape unlocked, so in we sneaked in without having to pay. I've got a feeling that I might be seeing a lot of films from now on. *Psycho* was rubbish, apart from the bit when the tasty bird gets it in the shower.

SUNDAY, AUGUST 2ND

Rehearsal day today. I only fluffed a couple of lines and without sounding like a big head I am so much better than all the others. The bloke playing Long John Silver does actually have only one proper leg so you would have thought that he might be used to moving around a bit as a uniped, but no he's crap. The whole thing resembled some sort of Norman Wisdom film as Sheila directed us all to shout 'bang' as we waved plastic toy pistols around. After about thirty seconds of this everybody just started laughing and Sheila ran off stage to sulk. Long John staggered after her, but alas she was long gone from Long John. I watched the news tonight to see if there was an item on Robert Louis Stevenson turning in his grave.

TUESDAY AUGUST 4TH

I started my apprenticeship yesterday, I am being taught by an old bloke called Keith who's about fifty and stinks of Old Spice aftershave. I spent most of the day watching him work and dodging the smells that were coming from his bum. The only good thing I will say about Keith is that he appears to be about the only bloke working here who hasn't shagged my mum.

THURSDAY AUGUST 6TH

An extra rehearsal tonight, we need it. Sheila has now dropped the 'bang' idea and she has now brought some plastic swords from Woolworth's. I was word perfect but all around me was cursing and chaos. The painters and carpenters here will put up the scenery on Saturday and we will rehearse again on Sunday. We perform to the old people on August 28th. They don't deserve this.

FRIDAY, AUGUST 7TH

I know I've only been doing this upholstery lark for a week but already I know it's not for me. Today I had a go at sewing some material to a bus seat, but after a minute or so Keith pointed out that I had sewn the material to the front of my boiler suit. Keith celebrated by laughing and farting at the same time. He really is very talented. I wasn't downwind so the joke was on him.

SATURDAY, AUGUST 8TH

Snuck in the Odeon this morning to see *Pollyanna*. After about ten minutes I realised that this was a girls' film. I suppose the clues were in the film's title. The actress called Hayley Mills was dead good though. I talked to a girl who worked in Timothy Whites, she was pretty although I felt stupid for not asking her name.

SUNDAY, AUGUST 9TH

The *Treasure Island* set looks great. Unfortunately it won't improve the standard of the acting. The mood of the cast is desperation and panic. Sheila actually said to me today that she wished I could play all the parts, I feel a bit sorry for her. She puts so much into the production only to watch a bunch of halfwits destroy it. Mum's out on the drink again tonight. I don't know where she gets the money from.

MONDAY, AUGUST 10TH

This upholstery lark is really getting on my nerves. Keith obviously knows that it's not for me and we both know that I'm hopeless at it. I can't do anything good with my hands that doesn't include thinking about girls and Sheila's tits. Keith's actually ok and as long as I put his horse racing bets on in the afternoons he's prepared to hide me for a bit while I carry on with the drama stuff. On the way home from work I brought some plasters from Timothy Whites just to see the girl I met at the pictures. I know now her name is Susan and she's a bit posher than me, well, at least she knows who her dad is and her mum's not a dirty old drunk. I very nearly asked her out but I panicked and then I ran off like some frightened hedgehog who'd just seen a group of hungry gypsies.

WEDNESDAY, AUGUST 12TH

I had a bit of money in my pocket today so I brought an LP from Woolworth's. It's called *Bridge over Troubled Water* by Simon and Garfunkel. I've no idea what it sounds like but I reckon that anybody called Garfunkel deserves a bit of money. I looked through the window of Timothy Whites and saw

Susan flirting with some really handsome bloke. He looked a bit like Roger Moore. I hope he's seriously ill and that she can't find his medicine. Sheila's getting really bossy with everyone except me, she's under serious pressure. Squire Trelawney didn't turn up tonight and to be honest we didn't miss him. Actually, things seemed to go a bit smoother. I pity the old people who will have to watch this rubbish. Hopefully, they might be all asleep by the interval, although the whole thing is taking so long they might actually have died by the end of act one. I got home by eleven and I heard a lot of moaning coming from mum's bedroom. She's in there with another one I suppose and I don't think that they are playing *Mouse Trap*, dirty old cow.

THURSDAY, AUGUST 13TH

As I suspected, there was another one at the kitchen table this morning. Mum didn't introduce him, I actually don't think she knew his name. It would be a lot easier if she gave them all squad numbers like the England football team, she could then put up a wall chart in the kitchen and keep track on them. Keith had a 12-1 winner at Kempton Park today so he let me go home early. I walked home via the canal and watched a bloke fishing for a while. Nothing happened. He could have been dead. I bought some more plasters today. Susan must think that I'm covered in the bloody things. I must ask her out soon or the government will start to ration plasters because I've got them all in my bedroom.

SATURDAY, AUGUST 15TH

I went to the pictures on my own today hoping to see my plaster girl. *Doctor in Trouble* was on and it was quite good although the cinema was nearly empty. I bet Susan went to Ealing to see the Beatles' film *Let it Be*. Mum actually stayed in tonight, she's probably having a rest before she goes out on the prowl again. I dreamed of Sheila's huge tits last night, I hope it's the same again tonight.

SUNDAY, AUGUST 16TH

The big day is getting nearer and my fellow twerps aren't getting any better. Squire Trelawney has returned. Apparently he had a sore throat and he lost his voice. Even though he has now found it he still can't remember when to say his lines. I'm definitely Sheila's blue-eyed boy, today I got a big showbizzy cuddle and I got a bit squashed up against those enormous breasts. I won't sleep well tonight, I might have to tie my hands together. Mum fell asleep on the sofa tonight. I don't think she's well.

TUESDAY, AUGUST 18TH

Finally, the plaster shortage has ended. I've asked Susan out. I can't believe that she only lives three streets away from me and that I've never noticed her before. I'm taking her for a Wimpy on Friday and already I'm dead nervous.

WEDNESDAY, AUGUST 19TH

I think I must be going crazy, I brought a single today called *Love Grows* by a group called Edison Lighthouse . . . why? I told Keith that I've got a date on Friday and he told me to make sure I've got a packet of French letters saying that I should get them from Timothy Whites because there's a cracking bit of crumpet that works there. I'm beginning to dislike Keith. There's definitely something wrong with mum, she was sick again this morning.

FRIDAY, AUGUST 21ST

I had a terrible dream last night that woke me up around two o'clock. In my dream I called for Susan and her dad answered the door dressed in a Klu Klux Klan costume. As Susan came to the door he said something like 'why couldn't you pick a white one?' She answered: 'He was the only one left.' This dream has done wonders for my confidence.

SATURDAY, AUGUST 22ND

So, Susan's dad wasn't dressed in all white with a pointed head. He was in fact a nice ordinary man called Ted who works in Safeway as a butcher. Her mum is called Val and is a stunner. She looks a bit like the girl in the Hai Karate advert, only older. She also has a younger brother called George named after her dad's favourite Beatle. I bet he's glad he didn't like the drummer. We went for a Wimpy and for a small girl she can't half eat and drink. I spent well over a pound. This afternoon we are going to Ealing to see *Let it Be*. I've told her that I want to be an actor. She didn't laugh which was good. It will be the first time in ages that I'll have to pay for the cinema, and for two people.Bugger!

SUNDAY, AUGUST 23RD

The film was great and we are going out again next week. I might have to have a re-think about her dad though. While we were snogging on her doorstep I saw him looking through the net curtains with a 'I don't trust that black boy' look on his face. Rehearsal tonight was alright until the twerp playing Bill Bones called Blind Pew, the Blind Jew. I think it was deliberate. Sheila's cuddling me a lot lately and it's getting a bit strange. She can't fancy me, can she?

MONDAY, AUGUST 24TH

Another Monday and another bollocking. The floor supervisor called me in to his office and then he cancelled my apprenticeship. This didn't surprise me or even annoy me. Evidently one of the canteen staff is knocking off a bloke who works in the betting shop and they reckon I'm in there more than the man who settles the bets. I can't complain. Keith was only doing his best for me. I'll miss his farting. I need to work here to stay in the drama club so I did a bit of apologising. Surprisingly, I was offered a job as a vehicle hygiene technician whatever that is. I said yes please, thank you, immediately.

TUESDAY, AUGUST 25TH

So I'm a fucking cleaner! Me and two other poor sods have to clean the buses once they come off the assembly line. I mean, how dirty can a brand new bus get? I'm on the inside and the other two idiots are doing the outsides. Balls to this, if this doesn't spur me on to leaving this place and to becoming an actor then nothing will. Went for another Wimpy with Susan after work tonight. She insisted on paying so I had an extra Bendy Burger and double chips. We had a massive snogging session. I'm not too sure about the tongue business though.

WEDNESDAY, AUGUST 26TH

It was dress rehearsal tonight, and my batty but lovely Auntie Joan made my costume because my mum couldn't be bothered. Auntie Joan cut the bottom off of some old jeans and stole one of my late Uncle Bill's checked shirts from his drawer and said: 'The tight old sod never wore it anyway.' Sheila was really pissed off tonight. Two of my fellow actors came dressed as Red Indians. Just the thing we needed when you're performing a play about pirates. I thought old people were supposed to be wiser than us young people.

THURSDAY, AUGUST 27TH

Mum's got to go into hospital for a couple of days with what she calls 'women's problems.' I thought that was when the twin tub wouldn't work. Auntie Joan will move in to look after me, so I should get a home cooked meal for once. I am worried about mum though, especially with the strain of the big performance tomorrow that I'm feeling.

FRIDAY, AUGUST 28TH

It's midnight and I'm back home in bed and the show is over. To be honest it wasn't the disaster that I thought it would be. There were a couple of forgotten lines and a mini collapse of scenery but the audience of about twenty five to thirty pensioners seemed not to notice. I think one of the old men must have pissed himself. Just before the interval there was a terrible smell coming from the tea trolley end of the stage, so our performance wasn't the only think that could have stunk the place out. I was very good, everyone said so although I don't think my performance deserved the massive kiss and cuddle that I got from Sheila. She definitely wants it. I'm seeing Susan tomorrow night.

SUNDAY, AUGUST 30TH

Last night didn't go to plan at all. Susan and me had planned to go to a disco but we ended up staying in all night. I reckon her dad watched us on the door step the other night and then he gave her a telling off. Had to sit on the sofa watching Morecambe and Wise and then a war film called *633 Squadron*. Her dad hardly saw any of it, he was watching me like a hungry dog watches a full can of Pedigree Chum. I'm beginning not to like him, but on the plus side, *633 Squadron* was a good film about planes and killing rotten Germans. I wonder if Susan's dad has got any German blood in him.

TUESDAY, SEPTEMBER 1ST

Mum came home today and she's very tired. I heard her say to Auntie Joan that her womb problem had been sorted out. Auntie Joan said something about her soon being back in the saddle again. To my knowledge mum has never shown any interest at all in horses. One of the bus seats had sick on it this morning and it was up to muggins to wash it off. This bus is brand new so one of the piss heads who works on the shop floor must have done it. I hate this job. Sheila sent a message to say that there's a meeting at five thirty tomorrow in the clubhouse and could all the drama club members attend.

WEDNESDAY, SEPTEMBER 2ND

So, the big news is that we are going to perform a pantomime near Christmas at George Tomlinson School. I called in to see Susan at lunchtime and she wants to go to a pub next week to see a group. I said: 'What will your dad, Adolf think of that?' She didn't understand or think it was funny. On my way home I got some abuse from a couple of skinheads. When I'm a famous actor those bastards will have to pay to watch me perform, if they're not in prison.

FRIDAY, SEPTEMBER 4TH

My name's in the local paper. There's a review of our performance in there and it says that I was dead good, well it says I was word perfect and that I had stage presence. Once she reads this then Susan must have sex with me. Before we go to the cinema tomorrow I'm taking her to my house to meet Mum and Auntie Joan. I must be fucking bonkers.

SUNDAY, SEPTEMBER 6TH

Well nobody will be in the slightest bit surprised to know that my mum has shagged Susan's dad! Is there any bloke living in Southall that she hasn't flattened some grass with. It turns out that they sat next to each other at senior school and shared a tent together on a school camping trip to Weymouth. What were the teachers thinking, when Auntie Joan told us Mum laughed, and Susan sulked all through *Ryan's Daughter*, as though the whole thing was my fault. It was also a big waste of a pound.

TUESDAY, SEPTEMBER 8TH

On my way to work this morning I sheepishly went in to see Susan. She was ok with me and said none of this was our doing. We will go for our usual Wimpy tomorrow after work and I'll pay. Both of the twits I work with, Colin and Dave, are off sick today so I got to play with the hose for a change. It's slightly less boring than the hoovering and polishing. Sheila announced tonight that the part of *Aladdin* in the pantomime will be played by Desmond. Nobody moaned, they'd better not. I'm beginning to really like Sheila now.

WEDNESDAY, SEPTEMBER 9TH

Old Adolf and Susan's mum were at bingo tonight so after a massive snogging session and a bit of a kerfuffle I managed to get Susan's bra off. Faced with those two lovely things in front of me, I suddenly realised that I didn't really know what to do, but after a bit of help from Susan I think I finally did ok. She knew what I wanted so after a bit of fumbling with my Tesco bomber's zip she did some handy work. I think I'm in love. I'm going to write a poem about her.

SATURDAY, SEPTEMBER 9TH

Poems are shit and hard to make up. I've tried but whatever I write just sounds rubbish so I've decided that chocolates speak louder than words. I'm going to buy Susan a box of Milk Tray. Auditions start tomorrow for the pantomime parts and even though I've already been cast Sheila wants me there. Anyway, I have a big part so I need to see what half- wits I'm acting with. Susan is at work all day today, and tomorrow she's at a family party. She wanted me to come but Adolf apparently said no. Mum seems a lot better. Tonight she came in at midnight from the pub, she was a bit drunk but at least she didn't have a hairy gorilla with her.

SUNDAY, SEPTEMBER 10TH

Only ten people turned up for the auditions this morning, we had hoped for new blood but no, the same old faces were there and I do mean old. Ted Rogers who works in the spraying department has to change glasses every time he reads from the script so the rehearsal is taking bloody ages. Doris Potter has got something called Parkinson's and she can't keep in one place for more than two seconds, and Bernard the uniped has got a new peg which looks six inches longer than his human leg. They must have knocked that up in the machine shop at work. By the end of the audition I had decided to throw myself off the railway bridge near the station or sling myself into the canal. Sheila had given us a cassette of the songs we had to learn so I thought I'd put all thoughts of suicide away for a bit. I'd never thought about having to sing before. I didn't have the guts to tell Sheila that we haven't got a cassette player at home. I'll have to buy one I suppose.

TUESDAY, SEPTEMBER 15TH

On my way back from borrowing a cassette player from the library I called in on Susan and I didn't like what I saw. She's got a new workmate called Jimmy and I don't like him. When I first got there she was giggling and playing with her hair like she used to when we first went out together. She introduced me as her friend not her boyfriend. Boy is only a three-letter word but it does make a difference.

FRIDAY, SEPTEMBER 18TH

Colin and Dave are on holiday. They have gone to the Isle of Wight Festival to see Jethro Tull, whoever he is. Things with Susan have cooled off a bit I think. She's never about when I call in the shop and a couple of times on Wednesday her brother said she wasn't in when I knocked on their door. I didn't believe him. If she's going to give me the brush off then I need to know so I can have a bash at Sheila. Mum seems to be back in the saddle already. Another uncle was here last night although I never saw him but I certainly heard him.

SATURDAY, SEPTEMBER 19TH

Disgusting! Mum's new bloke looks about seventy. It took him ten minutes to come down the stairs this morning. What does she do to them up there? Because of Susan's moods I have nothing to do today so I went up to my room to have a go at this singing lark. I'm glad I did because old man Steptoe and mum went back to bed for an encore. He sounds like one of the *Clangers*. What is she doing to him? This evening after her sexual assault course, Mum and me watched the *Black and White Minstrel show* on the telly. I read while on the bog last week that this is the most popular show on the telly. This must have been a misprint because it's shit.

SUNDAY, SEPTEMBER 20TH

With all the parts now cast for the panto today was meant to be the first serious rehearsal day, but of course things went wrong. The hall this morning was double booked. When I arrived I saw a load of old blokes playing skittles or something. After a lot of shouting and swearing by the old men and Sheila, the social club secretary decided that indoor bowls was more important than 'acting by a load of poofs and drama queen lezzers', so off home we went. It's no wonder that the BBC make awful programmes when drama clubs have to give way to a load of pensioners who only have weeks to live. When I arrived home there was a letter from Susan waiting for me. Auntie Joan called it a Dear Desmond letter. I didn't understand what she meant but then nobody does as she's a nutcase. Susan has broken up with me and she writes that she is too young for a proper boyfriend. No doubt next week I'll see the girl that is too young for a proper boyfriend wrapped around that git she works with. Let's see how he feels when he's spent a fortune on her and only gets a wank for his troubles. Its been an awful day so I'm going upstairs to learn my lines and try to sing. Tonight I shall dream about Sheila.

MONDAY, SEPTEMBER 21ST

Back at work this morning and apparently nobody here noticed that the Isle of Wight festival was in August, and in fact Colin and Dave were actually in court charged with possessing an illegal substance while in charge of a minor. It seems that they were both so doped up that they managed to leave Colin's five-year-old sister on the back of a 207 bus. Someone found her after she had slept the night in the bus depot. It's all going to be in the *Gazette* on Friday so the bosses here have sacked them before the whole of Southall sees it. So now I'm in complete control of the hygiene department which really means I get to use the hosepipe permanently. I've decided to walk over the other side of the pavement now when I go past Timothy Whites. Its got nothing to do with Susan. I just like looking at the dog shit on the pavement. I did however go into Woolworth's and buy *Tears of a Clown* by the brilliantly named Smokey Robinson. I heard it on the *Tony Blackburn Show* and it sounds dead good. Mum seems to have a bit more money, she doesn't work but this morning she gave me a pound to get some dinner.

TUESDAY, SEPTEMBER 22ND

More bad news tonight. Aladdin has been cancelled and the drama club has folded. Bad attendance and nobody staying for a drink has forced the social secretary to close us down. I'll bet he enjoyed it though. If you're not as drunk as a skunk and looking for a fight at kicking out time then they don't want to know you here. As I was beginning to go into a big sulk Sheila had a word with me about another drama club in Hayes.. It's a twice a week club and she will take me. She said that I was the only one in her class who was good enough for this new club, so that's nice. She said she would pick me up from work on Friday. I'm not sure I'm emotionally ready to share a car with a large breasted frustrated woman but I'll give it a try.

THURSDAY, SEPTEMBER 24TH

I went to the pictures on my own tonight to see *The House that Dripped Blood*. Christopher Lee and Peter Cushing were in it and they are supposed to be dead scary. They didn't scare me once, although it was good to get in to a X-certificate film without being stopped and asked my age.

FRIDAY, SEPTEMBER 25TH

After a long day playing with my hose, Sheila met me in the car park. She was wearing a really tight roll neck jumper that showed off her enormous tits. She looked a bit like an uglier version of Barbara Windsor. The drama club is based in the Hayes Community Centre and was called The Shining Star Club which sounds a bit queer to me. On the way there, Sheila explained that as well as putting on three shows a year they also provide people for crowd scenes on some film and television work. When we got there I met them all and joined in with some made up acting. Blimey, they were good. I'm not used to this, they were proper actors. The main man seemed to be a director called Ralph and I noticed that he couldn't keep his eyes off Sheila and that jumper. Sheila got a bit of a shock I think, and she quickly decided to concentrate on a backstage role for now, but not me, I can't wait to get started. Sheila dropped me off around ten o'clock and I thought for a split second that she might have wanted a quick snog, but I was dreaming, it was just my imagination.

SATURDAY, SEPTEMBER 26TH

This *Black and White Minstrel* thing is really getting on my nerves now, it's so bad but I just can't stop watching it. Why are they using white men pretending to be black men? I don't understand. One of the black/white ones actually said to another white one pretending to be Chinese 'My, it's good to see a nice clean face tonight'. Dick Emery was on afterwards and he was ok, the old woman who he dresses up like looks like my Auntie Joan and behaves like my mum when there's a man around.

SUNDAY, SEPTEMBER 27TH

I had arranged to meet Tommy Smith in the Wimpy before going to see a war film and Susan was in there with two of her friends. She saw me and waved, so I waved back and smiled, she's still dead gorgeous. I think Tommy thinks that we did it, because he keeps asking 'what was she like?' but I didn't answer him. I don't want Susan getting a bad reputation because of me telling lies. We sneaked down the alley and through the fire escape to see the film. It was called *The Last Grenade* and had Stanley Baker in it. He's a real actor, bloody great.

MONDAY, SEPTEMBER 28TH

It looks like old Nosey Parker, the careers teacher, might have been listening to me all along. This morning through the letter box dropped a load of stuff about acting and getting an agent. There was a big list of the best drama clubs around here and the one I've just joined in Hayes is one of the best. It might be a bit too soon but I might try and get an agent in a while.

TUESDAY, SEPTEMBER 29TH

At work today a new boy started, his name is Anthony and he went to Southall Grammar School, so he's probably a lot cleverer than me. So what's he doing cleaning buses then? To teach him a lesson for going to a grammar school I put him on the hoovering and then told him to get me a bacon roll from the canteen. No sign of Sheila tonight in the car park so I caught the bus to drama club. Ralph has cast me as a servant in a play that we are to do called *The Importance of being Ernest*. Ralph gave me a script and said, 'learn all your lines, darling.' It won't be hard. I've only fucking got four.

THURSDAY, OCTOBER 1ST

It's a new month so it's a new start. I am going to try and forget about Susan and I am also going to try and be nicer to mum even though I think that sometimes she's a dirty old cow. The gossip in the canteen is that Sheila and her husband Fred have separated. They say that he's been having it off with the Corona woman who comes twice a week. Sheila is not at work this week, she's on special sick leave apparently. Anthony broke another hoover today. For a grammar school boy he really is a spanner.

FRIDAY, OCTOBER 2ND

The drama group have received a letter from the *Carry On* team. They are looking for actors to appear in some scenes in their new film *Carry On Henry*. Filming starts on the 12th and they want as many bodies as possible. I will have to take a couple of days off work so I have put my name down on the list and want to do it for certain. I will call round and see Sheila tomorrow. This might cheer her up a bit. I just hope the Corona woman doesn't open the front door when I knock.

SATURDAY, OCTOBER 3RD

I chickened out of going to Sheila's house. I don't know why I just did. Instead I went to see *Carry on up the Jungle* at the Odeon and it was dead funny. The film is full of gorgeous women and I hope I see them all on the 12th. When I got home at teatime mum seemed to have another bloke in the house. She said that she had ordered us a bigger telly from Radio Rentals although I don't know how we can afford it. I went to bed and tried again to write a poem for Susan. I don't know why. I must just be missing her I suppose. Anyway, poetry's still rubbish and impossible to write.

SUNDAY, OCTOBER 4TH

Today's the day that I realised that I don't have any friends. I have nothing to do and nobody to do it with. It took me all of five minutes to learn my lines and I believe that I'm word perfect. I watched *Randall and Hopkirk*, and then *Please Sir* on the telly. There was a bit on the news about Janis Joplin dying. I don't even know who she is but the man reading the news said she was famous. *Please Sir* was funny and I wish I was in it. If I was I would definitely have a go at that Sharon bird.

MONDAY, OCTOBER 5TH
A real boring day washing buses and talking to Anthony. He is starting to grow on me now and he's ok. I was considering joining the camera club at work but then realised that I haven't got a camera so that's probably a no then. I waved at Susan tonight on my way home and she waved back. I thought about going in and buying some Hai Karate but then I didn't want to get back into the plaster situation again and buying Hai Karate is a lot more expensive than buying a stupid little box of plasters.

TUESDAY, OCTOBER 6TH
A new telly arrived this morning before work and it's bloody enormous and must cost a fortune to rent every week. Where are we getting the money from? Mum smokes like a chimney and drinks like a thirsty dog and she still seems to have money in her purse. Sheila was back at work and drama class tonight. She gave me a lift although we didn't say much on the way. She has dyed her hair red and somehow it seems to have made her tits even bigger. She is going to do the Carry-On thing. I might ask them to dress her as Little Bo Peep who was of course very

popular in King Henry's day. When I got home tonight I had a cold bath.

THURSDAY, OCTOBER 8TH

So, this morning there was a bloke called Sunil eating my boiled eggs. Auntie Joan called in on her way to Weightwatchers and said something about mum being a bit too loose, I don't think she was talking about her bowel movements. I had a think over my Rice Crispies and empty egg cup, and Auntie Joan definitely means that mum's a slag. Bloody Anthony called in sick today and I got lumbered with doing the whole lot, inside and out. I only got two done and I'm so bored with this job, all I can think about is escaping and going on to be an actor. I think I'm going back out with Susan again. When I walked past Timothy Whites tonight she came out and I think asked me out. We are meeting on Saturday outside the Havelock pub. She doesn't want her dad to know but I'll bet he finds out. Germans are good at getting information out of people.

FRIDAY, OCTOBER 9TH

I'm in a good mood today and I even brought Anthony a Curly Wurly from the canteen. Anthony's limping like Douglas Bader but I think he's pretending. He says he hurt his ankle playing football on Southall Rec, but nobody plays football on Southall Rec. There's too much dog shit on the grass. Sheila drove us to drama tonight and we all received the details about the Carry- On filming. Twelve of us have to be at Pinewood Studios for seven o'clock on Monday morning. We don't get any money for the two days, just free food and drink. Sheila will take the Vauxhall Viva and drive. She doesn't want to leave the car at home all day 'for that cheating bastard', her words not mine. I had a quick look in the A to Z to see where Pinewood Studios is. I still don't have a clue. Had a bath and washed my hair tonight, I have a big day tomorrow, I hope.

SATURDAY, OCTOBER 10TH

I was meeting Susan at two o'clock so why did I get up at eight this morning? Outside the pub when she came walking towards me I think that I had forgotten how pretty she was. We got the bus to Hayes and went for a Wimpy. She had a cheeseburger and chips which cost 4s 3d, and I had Bender the frankfurter and chips for 3s. She said that she has an interview on Thursday at EMI just down the road. She wants to train as a secretary and she's also hoping to see lots of pop stars. I told her about the Carry-On filming and she seemed dead interested. Her younger brother Tony got caught stealing some bath salts form Woolworth's last week. Adolf gave him a good hiding and stopped him going out at night for two weeks, a pity because he would have smelled nice. I said if she was nervous about the interview then I would go with her. She said thanks but it would seem a bit lame turning up with her boyfriend. We held hands on the bus and kissed outside the pub when we said goodbye. So is she my girlfriend again? Watched *On the Buses* and the *Ken Dodd Show* on the massive new telly last night. Not even having a new telly could make *On the Buses* any funnier.

SUNDAY OCTOBER 11TH

A boring Sunday learning my lines and I then went for a walk along the canal. Saw the same bloke fishing again. Is he dead? Mum gave me some money to get some food shopping. She's been out all day. Had a bath ready for tomorrow, no hot water again but I thought hot thoughts as I washed my nuts.

MONDAY, OCTOBER 12TH

Up early this morning to meet Sheila for lift to Pinewood. She's on time but does seem to have an awful lot of make up on. On the way she talked a lot about Fred and the Corona woman and I reckon if things fizzled out between them then she'd have him back, after first cutting his balls off. Well, making a film isn't what I thought it might be! After being shown into a large room we were fitted for our costumes. I was dressed as a beggar boy by a bloke who had a very high pitched voice. We were then walked outside to a large courtyard area with about fifty other people and told to stand behind a stage platform thing. We were then at various times, told to cheer and make a lot of noise like a bunch of idiots. We had something to eat, did the same thing in the afternoon and then we were told to get changed and told there's no need to come back tomorrow. Somebody said that Sid James and Kenneth Williams were there but I'm buggered if any of us saw them. What a disappointment and a complete waste of time. When I got home Auntie Joan was waiting for me. Mum's in hospital. She didn't come home last night and the police found her at two in the morning under the railway bridge. She has been beaten up and has cuts and bruises everywhere. Don our neighbour drove us to the hospital. She looks bad, and I heard Auntie Joan tell her 'you've got to give this lark up Beryl. The next time you'll be six feet under.' What a day!

TUESDAY, OCTOBER 13TH

A day off with nothing to do other than watch the schools programmes on the big telly. There was a programme about rocks followed by some pillock dressed as a clown dancing and singing like some halfwit reciting the alphabet. I almost wish that I was back at work. I went to Woolworth's after dinner to buy another pad for this diary and then said hello to Susan. I wanted to run up and snog her but I didn't want her getting the sack. She might need a reference if she got the job at EMI. Mum will be home later, so I went to the shops and brought her Ten Guards and a copy of this week's *TV Times* in the hope that she might stay in a bit now. As we were supposed to be at Pinewood today there's no drama club tonight. If the *Black and White Minstrels* are on the telly I might kill myself.

THURSDAY, OCTOBER 15TH

True Grit is on this week at the ABC in Ealing, so I will call in to see Susan to ask if she has heard anything about her interview and see if she wants to go. I love John Wayne, he may walk like his pants are too tight for him but he's a proper hero. Work today was so boring that I fell asleep on the back seat of a new 207. God bless Anthony for waking me up just as the yard supervisor was starting his inspection. Anthony deserves another Curly Wurly. Mum feels a bit better and she's starting to look a lot less like Henry Cooper, so that's good. My grandad rang Don next door to pass on a message to mum to say that he's coming down from Wales to visit her and then he's going to the rugby on Saturday. I don't mind him, although I remember he did call me 'Chalky' once or twice when I was younger.

FRIDAY, OCTOBER 16TH

Susan's cousins are coming down from Liverpool on Saturday so it's John Wayne day on Sunday now. She had a dream last night that during her typing test at the interview she typed tit instead of tight. She now thinks this might be true and that she did do it, but she also swears that she saw Paul McCartney coming out of a toilet carrying a mop and bucket, so I'm not taking her too seriously. She's coming here at twelve on Sunday, her dad still doesn't know about us being back together. Grandad Bill arrived this afternoon, he's English but supports Wales, my Auntie Joan says he should be hung on Tower Bridge for being a traitor. I don't really know him that well, he and Mum hadn't talked until I was about twelve and then Mum rang him because she wanted some money for our rent. I never met my nan although Auntie Joan said I missed out because she was the best one in my family, apart from her.

SATURDAY, OCTOBER 17TH

Grandad Bill slept in my room so I was on the sofa. After eating the biggest breakfast I've ever seen in this house, he left at ten to meet his fellow traitors at a pub in London. He'll be leaving for Wales after the game. Mum said it was hardly worth his while, all he did was eat her food this morning and drink her cherry brandy last night. I think she's forgotten about the money he gave her when she needed it. Watched *On the Buses* again last night, it's still not funny.

SUNDAY, OCTOBER 18TH

Susan arrived at one o'clock and she looked lovely. Despite mum knowing she was coming she made no effort to clear up at all, I had to hoover and clear up last night's mess. Unbelievably when I brought Susan into the front room Mum was cutting her toenails with her bare trotter up on the arm of our one only good armchair. Could she show me up any more than that?   After the film which was great, we had a big snogging session in the park until the park keeper moved us on for being an embarrassment to everyone for being too amorous, the miserable old git. Susan told me that she really likes a singer called David Cassidy. She saw a picture of him in Disco 45 and she thinks he's gorgeous. I've not seen him or heard him but already I hate him.

MONDAY, OCTOBER 19TH

Anthony and me got a big telling off this morning from Mr Roberts, a bigwig at work. It seems that the buses are coming back cleaner at night time once they have been used, than when they are going out in the mornings after we have cleaned them. I seriously need to leave this job, John Wayne wouldn't put up with this bollocks. I have written a letter to Hilary Tipping an agent in London who represents new young actors. I got her details from the stuff old Nosey Parker sent me. There's a disco at the social club on Saturday. I'll ask Susan about it tomorrow. I've managed to save over three pounds so I'll pay for the tickets.

TUESDAY, OCTOBER 20TH

We are going to the disco so I will get the tickets tomorrow at lunchtime. While we were getting told off yesterday I did say that we are still one person short and so today we got a new starter. She's called Peggy and she's only been here one day and already Anthony fancies her. She's tall, spotty and a bit dopey so she should be a good match for him. I thought all girls knew how to push a hoover around but Peggy doesn't know how to do it. This afternoon she got the hoover lead wrapped around her legs and she screamed for Anthony to help her. It might have been deliberate, she looked like a spotty Indian squaw that's been tied to a totem pole. I was word perfect at drama club tonight. I didn't need to look at my script at all and I think that might have cheesed off one or two of my fellow actors, but Jesus, I've only got four lines. Ralph calls everyone darling and I think Sheila's got the hots for him. On the way home it was Ralph this and Ralph that. I think he's a poofter and crosses the road from the other side of the bridge. I think I should tell her not to waste her time.

THURSDAY, OCTOBER 22ND

Good news today that Susan got the job at EMI, although it could be bad news for me that there's bound to be lots of really good looking blokes working there. She starts next week and she will go to college one day a week to do shorthand and other things. She told me today when I called in to pick up Auntie Joan's tablets to stop her falling over. Mum has things to help her fall over. They're called gin and cherry brandy.

FRIDAY, OCTOBER 23RD

Anthony has bought two tickets for him and Peggy, which is nice but he hasn't asked Peggy to go with him yet. He finally got around to it at lunchtime in the canteen. She went bright red but finally said yes. She's been walking around like the Queen of Sheba all afternoon. Tonight my mother who's back on the drink again actually found our kitchen. She made me a salmon paste sandwich and a packet of smoky bacon crisps for my tea. I saw an Arctic roll in the freezer bit of the fridge but mum couldn't be bothered to get off the sofa to get it. I know I could have done it myself but I had been at work all day not sitting around drinking. I haven't heard anything from Hillary Tipping yet she's probably really busy doing deals with Michael Caine and Oliver Reed.

SATURDAY, OCTOBER 24TH

It's early afternoon and I'm thinking about the disco tonight and I'm a bit nervous. I've only ever been to one disco before and that was at school and it was cancelled after an hour because Frankie Mullen set off the fire alarm half way through *Yellow River*. Tonight I'm sure will be better. I have a girlfriend, I will be smelling of Hai Karate, and I will look great.

SUNDAY, OCTOBER 25TH

God, I feel awful, my head aches and I think I've got the flu. Susan must have given it to me because last night we did a lot of snogging. She told Peggy last night that I am definitely her boyfriend and I'm her number one. Which now has got me thinking if I'm her number one how many more are on the list. Anthony and Peggy were like two limpets stuck together all night, and during *Bridge over Troubled Water* someone should have thrown a bucket of water over them. I walked Susan home at eleven but I couldn't come in because the big light was still on in her house. Mum came in about an hour after me and I heard her staggering up the stairs, at least she was on her own. I'm not well so I watched a musical on the BBC called *Oliver*, and *The Golden Shot* on ITV where surely it's only a matter of time before someone gets killed by a stray arrow.

MONDAY, OCTOBER 26TH

I didn't go to work today. I am too ill. Susan started work today and I said I would meet her at five o'clock at the EMI gate and go home with her. I look and feel like I've been jumped on by Giant Haystacks but I will be there. That's what number one's do.

TUESDAY, OCTOBER27TH

I met Susan yesterday and she was dead excited. She swears that she saw Paul McCartney again this time up a ladder mending some guttering. I'm going to have to tell her soon that there might be a handyman there that looks a bit like a Beatle. We went for a quick milk shake in the Wimpy but she had to get home to let her mum and Adolf know how she got on. Drama club tonight went well, it's all practice, practice, practice. My voice sounds ok but I'm not really a singer. Sheila is starting to get a bit embarrassing when she's around Ralph. She laughs out loud at his unfunny jokes and sticks to him like Bostik. Susan hasn't mentioned this David Cassidy person again, let's hope he's out of her system now.

WEDNESDAY, OCTOBER 28TH

I've just seen a picture of this David Cassidy in the *TV Times* and I've got to admit he's dead good looking. Even if I had a face transplant I'd never be as handsome as him. He's in something called *The Partridge Family* and the git can sing. I came home from work and I got a big surprise. Mum has got a real proper job. She is a packer at the Quaker Oats factory and says it's a lot of work for not a lot of money. Auntie Joan told her to have some pride and that 'she must be pleased not to be on her back twenty four hours of the day'. They then had a big row so I went to the chip shop for my tea. I heard *Band of Gold* on the radio tonight and I think I'll buy it tomorrow. My flu's gone I think and at least the massive boulder on my lip seems to be going.

THURSDAY, OCTOBER 29TH

Today I received a reply from Hilary Tipping. She said that she cannot take on new clients without a reference from a producer or director. I will ask Sheila for a reference, as she did direct us in the *Treasure Island* play. Mrs Tipping did say though that she liked my picture and would I possibly be interested in doing some modelling as she doesn't have any half caste boys on her books. I would rather do acting but if modelling would get me out of cleaning bloody buses then I'd do it. I will send her a reference and the clipping from the *Southall Gazette* straight away or as soon as Sheila does it. Mum hasn't been sacked yet. I'm seeing Susan on Saturday so this bastard thing on my lip had better be gone by then.

FRIDAY, OCTOBER 30TH

The Importance of being Earnest suddenly doesn't seem so important to two of my fellow actors. Two of the main characters have dropped out and the whole thing had to be recast. Ralph has offered me one of the lead roles although he's worried that I might be too young for the role. I must have sounded a bit big headed when I told him in front of the others that I would be fine and that I could handle it, no problem. So I'm going to play the part of Algernon.

SATURDAY, OCTOBER 31ST

What is it about girls? Susan was in a terrible mood today and completely bored with me after about half an hour, so I went home to learn my lines. I went upstairs to get away from the telly with a can of Tab and a Mars bar. There was a lot of noise about one thirty this morning when mum staggered in with another one. At least I didn't hear any Clanger noises.

SUNDAY, NOVEMBER 1ST

Another month and another uncle. This one's called Joseph and he works with my mum, so that didn't take her long did it? I'm not seeing Susan today. We are both better off on our own at the moment. I wonder how David pretty boy Cassidy would cope with her being so crazy. I watched *Bonanza* today. I wouldn't mind being in that. Do they have cowboys in England? Mum's new man left around three o'clock this afternoon after she said that they went back up to bed to read the Sunday papers. She must think I'm fucking daft. I know what they were doing, the dirty cow. We don't get any newspapers delivered on a Sunday. Had my dinner in my bedroom tonight, a packet of Spangles and a Crunchie.

MONDAY, NOVEMBER 2ND

Anthony is taking Peggy to the pictures this week to see the *Woodstock* film. I pretended to know what he was talking about hoping that he wouldn't ask me any questions about Woodstock. He said that Jimi Hendrix was one of his heroes and that he's so excited about seeing the film. I am such a spanner, I know nothing about this Jimi Hendrix fella, or even where Woodstock is. I looked it up later it's in Oxford. Tonight I found out a bit about Woodstock, it's a music festival. I wonder if Lulu or Cliff Richard are singing there. I'll ask Susan if she wants to see the film once she's better, but if the Partridge Family aren't in it then I don't suppose she'll go. Mum and Auntie Joan had another big row last night. I heard them downstairs.

TUESDAY NOVEMBER 3RD

Yes! Hillary Tipping wants to meet me. I only sent the stuff on Saturday so she must be keen. The agency is in London and I'm going on Friday. I will fake an illness at work after all I am an actor. I told Susan after work and she said that when I'm famous I can introduce her to David Cassidy. Well fuck that. She's obsessed with this little short arsed twerp. We are not going to the pictures this week, like me she's never even heard of Woodstock so at least we agree on something. I thanked Sheila for the reference and she said she's meeting Fred for a meal tomorrow. She said things with the Corona woman seem to be fizzling out. I thought of saying that perhaps she's lost her bottle but I thought better of it and kept my mouth shut.

WEDNESDAY, NOVEMBER 4TH

I lost control of the hose today and soaked myself. Fucking Anthony and Peggy pissed themselves laughing, the bastards. I hate this bloody job, and I must leave soon.

THURSDAY, NOVEMBER 5TH

There was a firework party at work tonight so I met Susan at the top of her road (her dad still doesn't trust me,) and we walked together holding hands. She was in a good mood and was really happy and she looked great in tight Levi's and an England rugby shirt. If things were different with her dad then I reckon I would have had a chance with her tonight, she's all touchy feely. The fireworks were rubbish, I reckon the bigwigs must have spent all of two pounds on two rockets and a couple of Roman candles. I will go next door and ring in sick tomorrow morning. I've got a big day in London with Mrs Tipping.

FRIDAY, NOVEMBER 6TH

Up early this morning and I caught the bus to Ealing Broadway station. I wore my best trousers that are actually my only pair of good trousers and my school blazer minus the badge. Hillary Tipping's office is on Wardour Street so I had to get the underground train to Leicester Square which is in London not Leicester. Walking down the road I saw my reflection in a shop window. Why did I wear my blazer? I look like a coffee coloured version of Just William. Hillary Tipping is a bloody bloke. As soon as he saw me he screamed: 'Oh my god, he's beautiful just like a young Kenny Lynch.' That's very worrying behaviour. After a quick chat he seemed to want to sign me on as a male model and he said he had work for me almost straight away. I told him that I really wanted to act but that I would be happy to start off doing some modelling work. Do I really trust a man called Hillary though? He talks like that Nancy boy on the *Dick Emery Show*.

SUNDAY, NOVEMBER 8TH

Sometimes I'm so bad at things that I can only laugh at myself. Susan, me, Anthony and Peggy all went ten pin bowling today and I was so bad at it that they all felt sorry for me. The only thing I will say is that ten pin bowling doesn't really count as a proper sport if you have to do it wearing clown's shoes. Susan's not keen on me doing this modelling thing for Hillary, she doesn't want other girls seeing my body. I said not to worry, when I should have said if she's all that worried about other girl's seeing my bits then it's about time that she had another look at them. But I didn't of course, just in case she dumps me again.

FRIDAY, NOVEMBER 13TH

There's been no diary for a few days but I've received a definite offer of work from Hillary Tipping. It will mean chucking in the bus washing and hoping I get enough jobs from Hillary. Auntie Joan says do it, Susan's sulking again, and mum's drunk as usual. I've just realised that today's Friday the 13th, what a day to make a career decision.

MONDAY, NOVEMBER 16TH

After a weekend of Susan sulking, today I handed in my notice. Only Anthony seemed bothered. I leave on Friday and I'll let Hillary know I'm available for work from next Monday.

TUESDAY, NOVEMBER 17TH

Susan has dumped me again, and I'm not bothered. She says that I don't respect her anymore, I suspect that she's got the needle about me doing the modelling but I can't help that. I'll miss her and her terrific bum a lot. I'll bet her dad's dancing on the ceiling, he will be so happy. Drama club tonight, and I made a lot of mistakes. This part of Algernon is very hard.

THURSDAY, NOVEMBER 19TH

I have heard from Hillary already. I have a job on Monday, I need to go to Denham airfield for a photo session for a girls' comic called *Jackie*. All I know is that I must be there for ten o'clock and I will be paid five pounds. During lunch I had a look at where Denham is. I can get a train to Uxbridge and then a bus, I hope. Excited, but also a bit scared.

FRIDAY, NOVEMBER 20TH

Today's my last day and not a single word from anybody other than Anthony and Peggy. I thought Keith might have made an effort, but no, I suppose I can't really complain too much I haven't exactly been a success here. Peggy gave me a sloppy kiss goodbye and Anthony gave me a handshake and a Mars bar. If I had to choose between the kiss, and the Mars bar then there is only one winner. I love Mars bars. I didn't go to drama class tonight, Sheila's on a second honeymoon in Blackpool with Fred and I couldn't be bothered to catch the bus. I'll learn my lines in my room tonight.

SATURDAY, NOVEMBER 21ST

I enjoyed *True Grit* so much the first time I'd thought I'd go again. Felt really sad that the last time I saw it Susan was with me, but she dumped me! If Lulu's not available in a couple of years then I might try and see her again. When I got home mum was watching *On the Buses*, no change, still not funny.

SUNDAY, NOVEMBER 22ND

Just when I need to be concentrating on looking all modelly for tomorrow, mum's in trouble again. She's upstairs in bed after being found last night blind drunk by PC Butcher. He said that she was importuning men in the pub toilets, but there won't be any charges because nobody wanted to do it with her. I looked up importuning in the dictionary and she definitely is a dirty cow. Once I become a rich model/actor, I'm moving out.

MONDAY, NOVEMBER 23RD

At ten o'clock this morning I entered a world that I didn't even know existed, and I loved it. At five to ten a lovely girl called Donna met me, dressed me and got someone else to style my hair. I then spent the next two hours with a gorgeous skinny girl called Rose. We had loads of pictures taken of us both standing in front of an old plane. I tried to chat up Rose a few times but I was back in the Susan dad thing again, as Rose's dad was there and he was watching me like a hungry hawk. After everything was finished and when I was waiting at the bus stop they drove right past me. I'm sure the bugger was smiling. I'll find out from Hillary as to when the pictures will be in the comic, so that's five pounds towards my moving out fund. A long day but loads better than washing buses.

TUESDAY, NOVEMBER 24TH

A quiet day today waiting for Hillary to let me know about any other jobs. I'm learning this Oscar Wilde play, it's hard and full of words that I don't really understand. At drama class I was a bit better, all because of my working at it today I suppose. Sheila still not here, she must be really getting it in Blackpool. Lucky Fred!

THURSDAY, NOVEMBER 26TH

Fuck Oscar Wilde, learning this play is ridiculous. PC Butcher called in this morning to tell my mum off, I think that she's way past telling off, she should be locked up. This afternoon I received a postal order for the Jackie job, it was for £5 less £2 for agent fees, and I haven't heard a bloody word from my agent. Auntie Joan has made me an offer, she has said that I can move in with her and her cat 'Hercules', I said yes please straight away and I shall tell mum once she has stopped smelling of Blue Nun and cherry brandy.

FRIDAY, NOVEMBER 27TH

We had the first proper run through of the play tonight and it went pretty well. My leading lady Cecily played by a nice girl called Julie is good and Ralph likes our 'chemistry'. To be quite honest, at times I haven't a clue what's going on but I listen and I seem to say my lines at the right time so at the moment Ralph's happy. I'm thinking of having a bash at Julie once the play is over, she's a bit older than me and is lovely.

SATURDAY, NOVEMBER 28TH

Back to normal today as me and Tommy Smith snuck into the pictures again through the fire exit. The film was called *Ned Kelly* and was a bit strange. It starred that ugly bloke from the Rolling Stones who I didn't know could act. Once it had finished we went into the Black Dog pub for a lager and lime. A regular, wobbly Paul told me that mum had been in since eleven drinking double cherry brandies, that didn't shock me. Tommy saw the chance then to tell me that Susan has a boyfriend called Alan who she works with. That didn't take long, did it? I asked Tommy if this Alan looked anything like David Cassidy, he said 'don't be stupid, nobody does'. I got home in time to watch a programme called *The Goodies*, all a bit silly and a little bit funny. Mum not at home, god knows where she is or what's she's up to. I move out on Monday to Auntie Joan and Hercules.

SUNDAY, NOVEMBER 29TH

Awake early this morning after a terrible night listening to my mother wailing like a sex mad baboon with somebody I think called Frank. I've decided to see Auntie Joan and ask if I can move in today I've had enough of living with a drunken nympho, especially when she happens to be my mother. *Randall and Hopkirk* was on the telly today, Marti's wife Jeannie is gorgeous and she has got me going a bit.

MONDAY, NOVEMBER 30TH

I moved in with my one suitcase full of clothes and my radio. To celebrate the move Auntie Joan cooked me Fray Bentos pie and chips. Lovely. Tomorrow night is our last run through before we perform on Friday. I'm ready but nervous.

TUESDAY, DECEMBER 1ST

Hillary rang Auntie Joan's and said he had got me an audition to do an advert for a deodorant called US. He said: 'I told them that you were gorgeous, darling and they were very impressed.' The audition is on Thursday morning at a studio in Shepherd's Bush so just a 207 bus ride then. Must learn my lines again for tonight.

WEDNESDAY, DECEMBER 2ND

That's it, no more rehearsals. On Friday about sixty people will pay four shillings each for the pleasure of seeing me perform. Last night went ok until Lady Bracknell fell over when someone trod on her dress. She cut her head on a stage light and then had to go to hospital for a stitch. Ralph was shitting himself but she turned up in the pub later and was ok. I sat next to Julie and I'm sure she touched my leg deliberately when she got up to go to the toilet. I think I'm in with a chance with her. Sheila's back and all loved up and has a massive love bite on her neck, at her age! I have my audition tomorrow and yet I'm not a bit nervous about it.

THURSDAY, DECEMBER 3RD

I think I will have to have a word with old Hillary. On arrival at the audition today I was met by a pretty boy called Julian who asked me what I wanted to sing as part of my audition. I said I didn't sing and that there's obviously been a mistake. After a minute or two of talking to the producer Julian came back and said: 'You've got the job, the producer thinks that you look like a young Kenny Lynch.' He also said that I would earn three pounds for two hours' work, so I said thanks. The advert will be filmed next week in time to be on the telly for Christmas, so that's exciting. Evidently my agent will let me know all the details early next week. I thought, you haven't bloody met him, mate.

FRIDAY, DECEMBER 4TH

I've done it. I am a virgin no longer. It's nearly three o'clock in the morning and about three hours ago I lost my cherry to my fellow actor Julie who it turns out is a very naughty girl. The play tonight was great. We all got what I'm told are two 'curtain calls' and Ralph says that I got a special cheer for being the only 'Darkie' in the cast. We all went to the pub and by eleven most of them were blind drunk. Julie asked me to walk her home as her house was empty because her mum and dad were in Kettering or somewhere like that. We fell onto her sofa and she practically attacked me, but it was brilliant. Do girls usually make that much noise? After she had finished with me, she ran to the toilet to be sick. Charming! Anyway, there was no lovey dovey stuff just a quick peck on the cheek and then my true love told me to clear off. I had to walk the three miles home running the risk of being attacked by the odd passing skinhead or Teddy Boy but it was worth it. I need to sleep. I'm now definitely a member of the Permissive Society and us playboys need to rest.

SATURDAY, DECEMBER 5TH

I had a bit of a lie-in this morning seeing as I had just had sex last night. I reckon Auntie Joan must have known something because she cooked me sausage, eggs and beans for breakfast, and she never does that. To celebrate my new found manhood I bought a Bob Dylan record called *New Morning* and played it on Auntie Joan's radiogram. It's fucking awful and bored the shit out of me. There was a review in the *Melody Maker* that said it would be the record to have over Christmas. The bloke who wrote the review must be crackers.

SUNDAY, DECEMBER 6TH

Went to see mum and pick up some more of my clothes. She looked a bit sheepish as if she has finally realised that being a bad mother is not a good thing. I read Auntie Joan's *News of the World* this afternoon. Apparently, decimalisation comes in next year. I wish I had paid more attention to Miss Reid in maths class instead of ogling Pauline Miles in her tight jumpers. What the hell is decimalisation? I went to the Wimpy at seven for my tea and I thought that I might be in a bit of trouble when two skinheads wearing silver Harrington's walked in. But I soon realised that it was Gay Gordon and his special friend Arthur from Southall Grammar School and they couldn't punch a hole through a jamboree bag. If Hillary Tipping doesn't get in touch by Tuesday then I'll ring him myself. I nearly had another try at Bob Dylan but Auntie Joan was watching telly when I got in, thank goodness.

MONDAY, DECEMBER 7TH

I caught a bus to W H Smith's in Ealing this morning and brought a copy of *The Stage* newspaper, I need to look for work and I seem to remember a drunken Julie say that the best place to look was in the Stage. When I got back to Auntie Joan's Tipping had left a message to say that the advert thing is mine on Wednesday in a warehouse in East Acton, so not too far to travel again. He also told Auntie Joan to say that I needed to be there by nine thirty sharp. I hope she's written the address down right.

TUESDAY, DECEMBER 8TH

Before drama club tonight I took Julie to one side with a view to asking her out, but before I could say anything she asked me if the other night was my first time. I lied and said no of course not. She said 'but you were crap at it though, my boyfriend can last for ages'. Well bollocks to her and she never said she had a boyfriend , and if I was so crap how come she made so much fucking noise and went off like a volcano. She said that perhaps we'd be better off being acting buddies from now on and if I ever meet her Eric then it's best I keep my mouth shut. Ralph got us messing around with Carols and things for a bit because on the twenty ninth we're doing a concert for the Rotary clubs of Southall and Hayes. I went home pissed off about Julie, and also with the tune of *When Santa got stuck up the Chimney*, stuck in my head.

WEDNESDAY, DECEMBER 9TH

The advert shoot was dead easy. I just danced around a bit in the background while some group who were supposed to be famous mimed to some old song. Lots of great looking birds there but not one of them wanted to talk to the boy who looks like a young Kenny Lynch. When I got home I rang another acting agency who are looking for young actors for a telly show. There might be a problem that they only want actors with Equity cards and I don't even have a Red Rover bus pass, but I am good at bullshit so that won't put me off. I bought *Band of Gold* by Freda Payne. Blimey, what a singer she is.

THURSDAY, DECEMBER 10TH

I've written a piece on Christmas for the drama club. Ralph had asked for ideas. It's a *Scrooge Christmas Carol* type thing only funny, and I've also learnt a bit from *Animal Farm* for this telly audition. So a busy day finished off with Auntie Joan's corned beef hash followed by *Arctic* roll and banana-flavoured ice cream.

FRIDAY, DECEMBER 11TH

That's it for me with Ralph and his stupid drama club. Three of us have taken the time to write some stuff for the Rotary show and he's decided to ignore it all and go with *Songs from the Blitz*. Well, he can piss off, I'm only fucking eighteen and you won't catch me singing bloody songs about packing up carrier bags and white rocks from Dover. It's Christmas or hasn't anybody told the old git. I was going to say goodbye to Julie but what's the point I'll never see her again anyway. I have an audition on Monday so I need to concentrate on that. It's nearly Christmas, how depressing.

SATURDAY, DECEMBER 12TH

I rehearsed my piece from *Animal Farm* over and over again today. It's really good. Auntie Joan's favourite Cliff Richard was on the telly tonight. His group were with him, and if that Hank Marvin bloke can get on the telly looking like that, then I reckon a good looking boy like me should have no trouble. To be honest though I must say that the ugly git can't half play the guitar.

SUNDAY, DECEMBER 13TH

Auntie Joan got a phone call from the police this morning. Mum has now been arrested for shoplifting. Could she get any worse? Unbelievably she got caught in Mothercare stealing a breast pump, she's nearly fifty years old, for God's sake. When the custody sergeant had stopped laughing he locked her up for the night, so this morning we went to get her out of jail. She was released without charge on account that 'it was Beryl again and she doesn't have a brain cell in her head'. On the way home on the bus she told us that she didn't really need the pump and she was 'borrowing it' for a friend. This is all too much worry for me what with my big audition coming up tomorrow.

MONDAY, DECEMBER 14TH

I was up at seven this morning in time to leave and catch two trains to Brentford for the audition. It was a strange place, a church hall near Brentford Football Club. My *Snowballs* piece from *Animal Farm* went well, I think. The place was packed with lovely looking girls and unfortunately for me even better looking boys. It turns out that this audition is for a radio show not a telly programme so being beautiful might not be so important, thank God. There was no mention of showing an Equity card so that was good. I came back and called in on mum with a small box of Milk Tray. She may be a drunk, thief, and a slapper but at least she's my drunk, thief, and slapper. She got a bit teary and told me to go into the kitchen and make myself a bacon sandwich but she didn't have any bacon, or bread. I'll go shopping for her tomorrow. I asked her if Frank, her new boyfriend, was around anymore. She said only when he wants a bit.

TUESDAY, DECEMBER 15TH

Hillary Tipping called to say that the deodorant ad is on telly tonight around seven thirty. I reminded him that he still owed me money. He said the 'cheque's in the post'.

WEDNESDAY, DECEMBER 16TH

If I'm ever in a police line- up, then the police would only need to show the witness the top of my head for them to shout, 'it was him'. That shitty advert last night showed the top of my nut twice and then concentrated on some ageing bloody made-up pop group. Auntie Joan called it 'a waste of your train fare, boy', and seeing as I haven't been paid yet, she might well be right. I've noticed that my old fella and my balls are itching a bit. I wonder if Auntie Joan has changed the washing powder that she uses.

THURSDAY, DECEMBER 17TH

I spent all morning putting up the Christmas tree and making soppy decorations to hang in the front room. A five pound postal order arrived from Tipping this morning. He's overpaid me but I'm keeping quiet. Fuck this itching, it's getting on my nerves.

FRIDAY, DECEMBER 18TH

Ace Academy left a message with Auntie Joan this morning while I was out and they want me to call them back at three. I've passed the audition and I've got the job. Brilliant! All the details will be sent to me, but I've just realised I'll have to let Tipping know that I've done the dirty on him. I've decided to be a coward and write to him. I never signed a contract or anything so things should be all right, I hope. I saw my advert again this afternoon during the break when *Crown Court* was on. I need a haircut. I need to see a doctor about my willie and balls.

SATURDAY, DECEMBER 19TH

Did nothing all day. No way for an eighteen-year-old to behave. Doctor's appointment on Monday at nine, there's definitely fire down below.

SUNDAY, DECEMBER 20TH

Did nothing but watch *The Golden Shot* and nobody's been killed yet.

MONDAY, DECEMBER 21ST

It's almost Christmas and Julie, the dirty girl, has given me crabs. According to Dr Secombe I'm covered in the little bastards. He reckons that there's so many of them that I should be charging them rent. He's so fucking funny. It's just my luck that when I have sex for the first time it would have to be with somebody who's obviously shagged as many blokes as my mum. Dr Secombe stabbed my willie like it was some undercooked sausage sitting in a boy scout's frying pan.

TUESDAY, DECEMBER 22ND

Sulking and scratching. Nothing else to write.

WEDNESDAY, DECEMBER 23RD

Dropping through the letter box this morning were Christmas cards and details of my radio show. It's called Drama Workshop and it's a school's radio programme. More details will be discussed on January 4th when I meet my new representative from Ace Academy. I will write to Tipping on Boxing Day. It seems right, he's bound to put up a fight.

THURSDAY, DECEMBER 24TH

A slightly less itchy trip to Woolworth's to buy Christmas presents. Bath cubes and a tin of Roses for Auntie Joan, and a box of Radox and After Eight mints for mum. She's coming here for Christmas dinner tomorrow now that Frank has left the scene of the crime. I possibly stupidly put a Christmas card through Susan's letter box this morning. It says 'I miss you'. I must be stupid. The tablets from the doctor seem to be working, tonight I'm hardly scratching at all.

MONDAY, DECEMBER 28TH

I don't want another Christmas like that ever again. It wasn't horrible just all a bit of a non- event. I must be the only person in England that doesn't like Morecambe and Wise, and I'm not in the slightest bit interested in what the Queen has to say. Mum was drunk all day on too many snowballs and cherry brandies and Auntie Joan spent most of the evening listening to her new Cliff LP that Pakistani Paul, her friend at bingo, had brought her. I went to my bedroom and ate a whole selection box and then felt as sick as a dog for the rest of the night. Auntie Joan did buy me a real good book on Charlie Chaplin though so I started to read that while waiting for the spots to appear from eating too much chocolate. Had a good check on my willie, things appear to be clearing up nicely already.

TUESDAY, DECEMBER 29TH

Tommy Smith got in touch today and invited me to a New Year's eve disco at the Gunnersbury Tavern in Ealing. I said yes straight away and then I went into Hayes to buy a Harrington from Millets. Mum had given me some money for Christmas but God knows how she earned it. I don't think that she's been to work for ages. With the price of the disco ticket I'm pretty much clean out of money for now. I spent the afternoon watching Christmas films on the telly, all a bit funny really when Christmas is now over.

THURSDAY, DECEMBER 31ST

It's New Year's Eve. I've had a good old inspection down below and things are looking all mended. I reckon that if I have half a chance with a desperate drunken girl then I should have a bash at another bunk up. I had a nice long bath and slapped on plenty of Hai Karate ready for action. Auntie Joan lent me two pounds for tonight. I met Tommy and his mate Ian in the pub and I felt that tonight was going to be a really good night, then as usual disaster strikes. Mum has had a heart attack and is on her way to hospital in an ambulance. She's my mum and I feel so sorry for her, but why tonight? I went home and Auntie Joan and me got a taxi to the hospital at about the same time that I should have been going in a taxi to the disco. When we went into casualty mum was lying there hooked up to a drip, I suppose that makes a change from her being hooked up to a bottle of Blue Nun. She looked terrible and kept moaning about being sorry as she drifted in and out of sleep. For the first time ever I think, I actually felt sorry for her. Auntie Joan and me stayed with her until she was out of danger and then we came home at about two in the morning. Happy fucking New Year!

NEW YEARS DAY, 1971

Mum was moved to a side ward at six this morning and she's definitely out of danger. She got a right telling off from a doctor. She must stop drinking and get more exercise and that doesn't include sitting on top of hairy arsed men that she's just met. Auntie Joan made me eggs on toast this morning, she's just how a mum should be. Tommy Smith rang to see how mum was and to say that Susan was there last night looking great and asking all about me. He also said that he shagged a girl called Felicity but he's lying. No posh girl called Felicity would shag an ugly git like him no matter how desperate she was. I will go and see mum again tomorrow afternoon. I had a final inspection down below tonight while I was having a fumble, all back to normal and working well.

SATURDAY, JANUARY 2ND
I read the letter from Ace Academy again to try and work out the best route to Turnham Green which sounds a bit like my willie and balls over the past week. It seems like mum's heart attack was quite a big one, she's dead lucky still to be here. A lovely nurse called Barbara smiled at me in a real sexy way. Well, I was wearing my Harrington and lots of Hai Karate.

SUNDAY, JANUARY 3RD
Nothing much today except watching *The Golden Shot*. Still nobody killed yet. I wouldn't mind having a bash at that Anne Aston bird though. A Sunday bath ready for my meeting with Ace Academy tomorrow.

MONDAY, JANUARY 4TH
Today's meeting with Ace went well and could be well exciting. A very camp fella called Lucien, (really) introduced himself to me and told me I'm gorgeous. He seemed harmless enough though. Lucien had seen me on the cover of *Jackie* and was

prepared to give me some work almost straight away. A new British film to be filmed at Elstree studios wanted good looking blokes for what Lucien called background shots. I told Lucien that I didn't have an Equity card but he wasn't worried and said that he'd deal with it. The brightly coloured Lucien had a standard contract printed up already and hurriedly and possibly stupidly, I signed it. Filming starts on the eleventh and whatever happens I've gone and done it now. I don't even know anything about the money. Ace Academy will send on the details. Exciting but also a bit worrying. I called in to see mum on the way home. She already looks a bit better and can be dead pretty when she's not on the drink. Barbara the nurse is well friendly, she's a lot older than me but I've decided that I'm going to ask her out. Very soon I will be riding her like Lester Piggott.

TUESDAY, JANUARY 5TH

It seems that Barbara is in fact twenty six and married to a train driver called Len, but that doesn't seem to worry her at all. Over a can of Tab and a Kit Kat in the hospital canteen she told me that Len is a bully and that she would love to go out with me. She's available on Saturday night as Len is on late shift and that means that she will have the car. We will have to meet in Hounslow so nobody sees us. We are meeting outside the Bell pub at seven and I'm excited and horny.

WEDNESDAY, JANUARY 6TH

I had a bit of money left from not going to the New Year's Eve disco so I bought a new Brutus shirt. I wanted a Ben Sherman but I couldn't afford it. I might ask Auntie Joan for another loan on Saturday seeing as I'm going to be sleeping on the sofa for a bit. Mum's being released from hospital and like a naughty schoolgirl she'll have to stay with a responsible adult, so Auntie Joan's got the job. If it keeps her off the Blue Nun for a while then that's good.

THURSDAY, JANUARY 7TH

The copy of my contract arrived this morning along with the details of the film shoot. For a couple of days' work it says I will get seven pounds plus possible extra money. The film is called *Percy* and will be an X certificate so it might be a bit scary. I'm to report to Betty the producer . Filming starts on Monday at eleven o' clock. There was also a handwritten note from Lucien that said that my Equity card would be ready in a week and that I should enjoy the shoot. How did he do that?

FRIDAY, JANUARY 8TH

We collected mum from hospital this morning and she seems a bit quiet and a bit too calm. I reckon she might have been tranquilised like the way they shoot lions before a vet needs to fix them. She went straight up to my bed when we got home and when Auntie Joan unpacked mum's bag she found a copy of the Bible. I said it would be great if Mum had stopped all her nonsense and had found God, Auntie Joan said: 'Best check the Bible to see if the pages have been cut out to hide a bottle of gin inside it.' I do hope that she's found Jesus, although I think he liked a drink occasionally.

SATURDAY, JANUARY 9TH

I had a bad night's sleep on the sofa. When I did drop off I had a dream that Barbara's husband Len caught us shagging and cut off my balls with a meat cleaver. Not really the sort of thing that you want to dream about eight hours before a date with a dead sexy nurse.

SUNDAY, JANUARY 10TH

Last night I had sex with a married woman on the backseat of a Vauxhall Viva, and it was FANTASTIC.

MONDAY, JANUARY 11TH

1. Today I met George Best.
2. I was stark naked in a shower with five gorgeous girls.
3. I'm definitely shit at football.

Percy is basically a mucky film about a man whose had his willy cut off by a big pane of falling glass. He then has a willy transplant. I can't tell you anything else about the film because at the end of the day's filming Betty decided that they didn't have the budget for me and two of the girls tomorrow. I don't care. I got three pounds dressed in football kit and another two for being bollock naked in the shower. I'm not exactly proud of what I've done but I like the money, and I did meet George Best. I'm pretty sure Michael Caine started off doing stuff like this, didn't he?

TUESDAY, JANUARY 12TH

Someone found a bit of dignity and pulled out of filming

today so I'm back in. I stood around for most of the day in the freezing cold on an icy football pitch trying to avoid the ball. An actor called Hywel Bennett was the star today and a right miserable sod he was. I did however get a sneaky look at a half-naked actress called Elke Sommer and she's fucking gorgeous.

WEDNESDAY, JANUARY 13TH

I rang Barbara when she was at work this morning. All she said was 'same place same time tomorrow.' I think she might be using me just for her pleasure.

THURSDAY, JANUARY 14TH

I'm lying on the sofa after another quick one with Barbara. Surely I can't stay this lucky, a shag, lift home, and only spent a pound. Ace have been in touch again, more work coming up on a film called *Please Sir*, from the title I'm already a bit worried about it. I'll ring Lucien tomorrow.

FRIDAY, JANUARY 15TH

Lucien wants me to come in on Monday. He has my Equity card and an idea to put to me. *Please Sir* isn't another mucky film, it's a spin off film from the TV series about a school. I have another non- speaking part and I forgot to ask about the money. Mum has really changed. Auntie Joan says that she won't even suck a wine gum now, which makes a change from some of the things she's probably had in her mouth lately. She went to a coffee morning at St John's Church today. It won't last. Len's on nights again on Sunday, so Barbara wants a seeing to. I saw a group called T-Rex on the telly tonight, the singer looked dead good but I'm not sure if it was a boy or a girl. It sang a song called *Hot Love* and I thought about buying it for Barbara, but if Len finds out, my meat cleaver dream might just come true.

SATURDAY, JANUARY 16TH

A quiet day in, saving some energy for Barbara. Mum's at church arranging the flowers. Auntie Joan is still very suspicious of the whole 'changed mum thing.' She has now locked up the sherry and cherry brandy and keeps her purse always within three feet of her wherever she goes.

SUNDAY, JANUARY 17TH

Met Barbara outside the Bell and she drove us to Hounslow Common where she interfered with me twice. She's great.

MONDAY, JANUARY 18TH

This morning Lucien introduced me to Sven who handed me a brand new shiny Equity card. It looked a bit like it had just been printed by one of those John Bull printing machines but good old Sven said it was the real thing. Lucien then said that Ace Academy had decided to 're-invent' me, which basically means that they want me to be called Dessie Twelvetrees instead of Desmond. I suppose it doesn't sound too bad, James Bond starring Dessie Twelvetrees. I quite like that. Sven had a big girlie cuddle with Lucien when he left. I think he's a bit funny as well. For three days' work at Pinewood studios I will be paid twelve pounds, not a lot of money really but it's a proper film and I don't have to show my bum to anyone.

TUESDAY, JANUARY 19TH

This morning Auntie Joan found a French letter in the pocket of my dirty Levis, thank God it was still unopened and in the packet. She made a big point of giving it back to me saying that 'it only seems a minute ago that you were still doing Noddy jigsaws'. I daren't tell her that it was bought for me by the married nurse who looked after mum. Later, I had a nice night out with Tommy. I told him all about me and Barbara but to be honest I don't think he believed me. He said that Susan had been dumped again by someone she worked with called Kevin. She only dumped me in November. Mum's going around Southall selling copies of *The Watchtower*. Auntie Joan's swears it's because that includes going in and out of pubs all night.

WEDNESDAY, JANUARY 20TH

Today was the first day of the *Please Sir* film shoot and that meant lots of standing around eating greasy bacon sandwiches from a catering van. About twenty of us were filmed in the afternoon getting on and off a coach, and occasionally being asked to make a lot of noise. The point of the film is that everyone from the school is on a camping trip. Tomorrow we are supposed to be having a big fight with kids from another school. It's a long day but at times it was a lot of fun, and the food is brilliant. I've never eaten so much. I've not heard from Barbara for a couple of days, Len must be off work.

THURSDAY, JANUARY 21ST

Arsed about all day supposedly fighting with a lot of posh kids dressed in red blazers. They came from an acting school in Croydon and were a little bit too cocky for my liking. Isn't Croydon a dump? Three more bacon sandwiches and a steak and kidney pie today. If this carries on I'll soon be the size of Giant Haystacks. I know it's early days but I could really do with a speaking part. This is all a bit too easy. I want to do some proper acting. Auntie Joan and mum have had a big argument. I don't know any facts I just know that Auntie Joan told mum to 'sling her fucking hook'. So at least I'm back sleeping in my own bed again.

FRIDAY, JANUARY 22ND

Part of my acting today was that I was asked to touch a girl's bum. Her name was Jenny and she was lovely. In the afternoon over yet another bacon sandwich she gave me her phone number. She said I remind her of that singer Kenny Lynch. If I don't hear from Barbara again then I'll give Jenny a call and she can see what Kenny Lynch might do for her.

SATURDAY, JANUARY 23RD

Today I saw a proper actor, Peter O'Toole in a film called *Murphy's War*. After the film I went to the Wimpy to see if anyone I knew was there, but as I was eating my egg burger I actually realised that I only really ever have had two friends, Tommy Smith and Susan. Feeling a bit low again as I write this.

SUNDAY, JANUARY 24TH

After a night of feeling sorry for myself I decided that today would be 'be nice to mum day', so I decided to spend the day with her. I must have been mad. The day started with a visit to church of course. Things happened but I didn't understand a word of what went on. Then she took me to the local Scout hut where she served tea and fig roll biscuits to a load of smelly pensioners who all seemed to get the fig rolls stuck to their false teeth. I told mum that I didn't feel well around about twelve o'clock and I ran away like the loyal son that I am. I now know what happened between mum and Auntie Joan. While Auntie Joan was out shopping mum brought Vince the local tramp home for a bath and something to eat. After Vince had finished his bath, Mum gave Vince one of my dead grandad's suits to wear from auntie's wardrobe. As my auntie came in from shopping she looked up and saw what she thought was her dead husband coming down the stairs holding her daughter's hand. She nearly had a heart attack and died at the bottom of the stairs. I can't really remember my Grandad Wally, but judging from the state of the suit he must have been a scruffy old bloke.

MONDAY, JANUARY 25TH

To be fair to Lucien, he is trying to get me work. After I had a talk with him, he rang to say that I have an audition for a stage play on Thursday. The play is called *A Raisin in the Sun*, Lucien said to go to the library and get the book out. I'm to read for the part of Travis. Still no word from Barbara so I might ring her tonight and see if she's at work.

TUESDAY, JANUARY 26TH

Fuck, this book is hard work. It's about a black family so I might stand a chance if I can understand what's happening. On the cover of the book this Travis looks about twelve so that's not very encouraging. I've tried all day to understand it but it's about as believable as those young girls fancying those old gits in that *On the Buses* programme.

WEDNESDAY, JANUARY 27TH

I'm trying really hard to sound American as I read this book aloud today but I think I just end up sounding like Benny out of the *Top Cat* cartoon. I won't get the part but I will go anyway, it's in somewhere called Bushey wherever that is. Looked in the A to Z tonight and I still don't know where Bushey is. Will get a train to Watford and walk. Auntie Joan's still annoyed with mum and only talks to her occasionally.

THURSDAY, JANUARY 28TH

Two trains and one bus took me to Bushey Community Centre. As I got there another guy who I know now is called Sean was outside having a fag. He said he was here to audition for the part of Travis but he had no chance as he didn't understand a word of it. For once, I kept my mouth shut. I think the audition was a bit of a disaster. Halfway through my reading to a table full of big wigs I suddenly realised my accent had gone from Top Cat to Tommy Cooper. I might just as well have been wearing a fucking fez. Once the whole thing had finished I went to a café with Sean and we swapped telephone numbers. Who knows we might meet sometime in the future on the set of a new James Bond film.

FRIDAY, JANUARY 29TH

Anthony got in touch today and said that there's a disco tomorrow at the AEC and did I want to come. I said yes straight away. I really need to get out of the house at nights. God knows I could do with cheering up, I've got no job, hardly any money and Barbara seems to have used me as her sexual plaything to have and then throw away. It was good hearing from Anthony again. He and Peggy are well in love. There's obviously a lot to be said for going out with a nice plain girl. I thought about ringing that girl Jenny from the *Please Sir* film, but I'm not sure taking her to a factory works do would make a good impression on a budding young actress.

SATURDAY, JANUARY 30TH

All Hai Karate'd up and ready to go. I will enjoy tonight.

SUNDAY, JANUARY 31ST

So, Susan and me are back together again. I hadn't a clue that she was going to be at the disco but Anthony and Peggy obviously did. Susan is still absolutely lovely and the bonus is that she has gone off David Cassidy after reading that he's having a fling with the girl from the Partridge family. I've just got enough money to take her for a Wimpy this afternoon if she doesn't eat too much. She's still working at EMI but hasn't seen anyone famous apart from someone who presents *Blue Peter* who was walking down a corridor looking for a lost dog.

MONDAY, FEBRUARY 1ST

Another month and thank God another phone call this morning from Lucien. Surprise, surprise I didn't get the part in the play at Bushey, but the production company that made *Percy* have a part for me in another mucky film. I don't want to do it but it's twelve pounds and I'm broke, and I also have a hungry girlfriend. If anybody asks then I'm doing an advert that's going to be shown only in Germany, that should do the trick. Lucien will send me details tomorrow. I can't wait !

TUESDAY FEBRUARY 2ND

I'm not sure why but when I called for Susan tonight her mum and brother were nice to me. Her brother Tony hasn't changed much. He's still a scruffy twerp who could do with a good bath. Susan said she'd pay tonight so we caught a bus to the EMI social club so she could 'show me off', to her friends. As it turned out there were only three people in there and that included the fat bloke who worked behind the bar. Still it was nice to be together again. We had a bit of a snog in the corner and when I got up with Susan's money to get the drinks I had a stiffy on that was the size of the Post Office Tower. I told her that I had just got an acting job in an advert for German television, she asked me what I was advertising and I panicked and said Spam. What a tosser I am sometimes. Had a massive snogging session again on her doorstep later and the Post Office Tower showed up again.

WEDNESDAY, FEBRUARY 3RD

Auntie Joan is getting in a right old state about this decimalisation that's coming in soon saying stuff like 'Ten bob will always be ten bob to somebody as old as me and no frog or wop is going to change that.' The script came today and it's called *Secret Rites* and it seems like I have to dance around a camp fire bollock naked pretending to be happy and for that I will get twelve pounds and a cold arse. Filming is in a studio in Wardour Street in London and they want me on Monday. Susan and me are going to see a new group perfom on Friday. She's paying again.

THURSDAY, FEBRUARY 4TH

I felt a bit guilty today. Hillary Tipping sent me two pounds for the radio play audition I did ages ago. He didn't have to do that, and I'm dead lucky that I don't have to pay Auntie Joan any rent.

FRIDAY, FEBRUARY 5TH

Mum has left Auntie Joan's for good and is now living with Vince, the tramp. Can she be any more embarrassing?

SATURDAY, FEBRUARY 6TH

Susan and me went to the Hamborough Tavern last night to see a group called Spider. They were dead good. Her workmates were there, two good- looking girls called Sally and Jackie. Jackie had a boyfriend called Todd who looked a bit like that weirdo singer Tiny Tim. The tight bastard didn't buy a drink all night, I'm sure he went home with more money than he came with. Spider played what was called heavy rock music and it was loud and fast. Lots of kissing and touching on the way home last night. I reckon it won't be long.

SUNDAY, FEBRUARY 7TH

Trying to make things better with Auntie Joan, mum has invited us over for Sunday dinner. As I write this now I'm thinking that I'm probably going to be writing something bad tonight after the last supper with the lady and the tramp. Back home now and I'm happy to report that we made it through the afternoon. Vince is actually quite a nice bloke who just seems to be a bit down on his luck after his wife walked out on him. Things didn't get off to a great start when mum made everyone say the Lord's Prayer before we had our prawn cocktail. Dinner was a bit burned but it was possibly the first time mum has cooked anything since I was about ten. We had burned chicken, peas and Cadbury's Smash. There was lots of talk about finding God. Auntie Joan whispered to me that it would have been better if mum had gone into the kitchen and found some pudding. She also said that the 'tramp will soon get fed up with all this God talk and will be sleeping in the doorway of the Co-op next week'. We went home after *Songs of Praise* on the telly and Auntie Joan opened a tin of pears and evaporated milk. I hope Vince doesn't disappear, I quite liked him.

MONDAY, FEBRUARY 8TH

I will never do a film shoot like that again. I'm too embarrassed to even write about it. If that film ever gets released in this country then I'll have to move to Australia. I am going to get a proper job. I don't want to but I won't go through something like that again.

TUESDAY, FEBRUARY 9TH

Auntie Joan's next door neighbour has got me an interview with someone called Mr Compass at Quaker Oats this afternoon. I've no idea what the job is but it can't be anywhere near as bad as what happened to me yesterday.

WEDNESDAY, FEBRUARY 10TH

Apparently, I'm not even qualified enough to pack fucking boxes of porridge. The idiot called Compass said that I don't have the necessary experience to work as part of a team. But like some sort of miracle a toilet cleaning job has just become available. I said bollocks and walked out once Mr Compass had pointed me in the right direction.

THURSDAY, FEBRUARY 11TH

After a terrible night's sleep I asked Lucien's secretary for a meeting. She said that he wasn't in the office today but that's bullshit. I will keep on ringing until Auntie Joan tells me to stop making phone calls. I saw Susan tonight and told her all my problems but not what happened on the film shoot. She was dead nice and on her sofa later she let me take her bra off.

FRIDAY, FEBRUARY 12TH

This decimalisation thing starts next week and Auntie Joan is in a right state. She's blaming the French and their stinking garlic. It won't bother me, all I need to know is ten bob will now be fifty pence. That's all I ever have in my pocket anyway. Lucien rang this afternoon and said I'm not to worry and that he's sent me something in the post and it should be arriving tomorrow morning.

SATURDAY, FEBRUARY 13TH

I had a real stroke of luck this morning. Through the letter box dropped an envelope with love from all at Ace Academy on it. Inside are two tickets for a film premiere for tomorrow night. The film is called *10 Rillington Place* and they will make the perfect Valentine's Day present for Susan tomorrow. I don't think I'll say anything to her about them being sent by Lucien, I'll just tell her I got them from one of my actor friends. I need to ring her soon as this might be a dressing up thing. Susan was excited, she's going to Wembley market tomorrow morning with her mum to buy a new dress. I'll be wearing my old school trousers and my Brutus shirt if Auntie Joan will wash them.

MONDAY, FEBRUARY 15TH

Last night was the best time ever. The film was brilliant, Susan looked gorgeous and I had the best Valentine's present ever. When the film ended and we were on our way back to the station Susan whispered that she had a surprise for me. She told me that instead of going home we were going to a hotel. I had a whole night with my lovely girl. If her dad ever finds out he'll bloody kill me. She has an alibi and her mum will back her up, bless her. Found out today that a 2/6 bus fare is now 12p. Doesn't seem right to me somehow.

TUESDAY, FEBRUARY 16TH
So, Susan's alibi lasted all of one bloody day. Her stupid workmate Sally forgot all about the fact that Susan was supposed to be staying at her house on Sunday night and rang Susan's house just as *Coronation Street* had finished. Of course her dad answered the phone. There was a big argument and Susan's mum had to come clean. This is almost certain to be my fault. I did however receive news from Ace that I had got a read through on Friday of a stage play called *The Basement.*

WEDNESDAY, FEBRUARY 17TH
The script for the play came this afternoon by special delivery and it's in Manchester which is like the other side of the world. There's tons to learn but it all looks good. I tried to get hold of Susan at work today but I was told she wasn't in. Her dad has probably locked her in her bedroom and is sticking pins into a half caste Action Man doll.

THURSDAY, FEBRUARY 18TH
In bed all day learning lines. I have to be up at five in the morning to catch the train to Manchester. The directions from Ace are pretty good and I should be there for eleven o'clock. I rang EMI again today and that dopey cow Sally said Susan

had the flu. I couldn't be bothered to talk to her about Sunday. When I get home tomorrow night I'll go round to see how she is and let old Adolf thump me.

SATURDAY, FEBRUARY 20TH

Thanks to London Transport I missed the bloody train by five minutes and arrived at the read through nearly an hour late, but everyone was ok about it. I think I impressed them because I was word perfect and Felicity, the boss of the Noon theatre company, said she was pleased with me. She also said that she thought she recognised me from somewhere. I hope it wasn't from that mucky film I did. I didn't go to Susan's. I was too tired to get beat up and spend the night in casualty.

SUNDAY, FEBRUARY 21ST.

I plucked up the courage and rang Susan's house. Thank God she answered. She's allowed out today and she's well enough to go back to work tomorrow. We are meeting at the Wimpy at four. She says her dad definitely blames me and perhaps we should meet in secret again for a while. I don't mind, I actually would like to keep my knackers a bit longer. Susan told me that her mum and dad haven't spoken for a week now, all because Susan could no longer resist me.

MONDAY, FEBRUARY 22ND

I'm reading a book called *The Exorcist* and even though it's scaring the shit out of me I can't stop reading it. I woke up last night sweating like I'd just done ten rounds with Big Daddy.

TUESDAY, FEBRUARY 23RD

It seems like my girlfriend has really got the hang of this sex thing now. On the way home from the pub tonight she dragged me into the cemetery and shagged me. It was great but I'm not very proud of myself for having it off in a cemetery. There's nothing clever in having 'in loving memory' pressed into your bum.

WEDNESDAY, FEBRUARY 24TH

I always seem to get good news followed by potential bad news. I have passed the audition in Manchester and Lucien has said the part is mine if I want it. The money's good but the bad news is that I will be away for four weeks while we take the play to the clubs around Manchester. I've never ever been away from home before apart from that dirty night in the hotel with Susan, and she's not going to be happy either. Rehearsals start next week and I've got to do it. This is proper acting and it's what I've been waiting for.

THURSDAY, FEBRUARY 25TH

Details about the play should arrive tomorrow. I told Lucien yes and he seemed dead happy. Now to tell everyone else. Auntie Joan might worry about me, Susan might cry about me, and Mum might pray for me. *The Basement* is about two blokes living together and I'm playing Tim one of the main characters.

FRIDAY, FEBRUARY 26TH

Started to learn lines today. Going out for a last meal with Susan tomorrow. She hasn't taken the news all that well but she says her dad is walking around like he's got eight draws up on the pools. Evidently, he told his family around the breakfast table this morning about an episode of *Bonanza* where an Indian brave had to tell his squaw to forget him and find someone else while he was away fighting cowboys. The man's a wanker.

SATURDAY, FEBRUARY 27TH
Line learning, bath, Hai Karate and then dinner at the Berni Inn with Susan and hopefully cemetery sex.

SUNDAY, FEBRUARY 28TH
Not a great night last night, Susan being a bit sulky and childish. I'm going for four weeks not four years. A real big Sunday dinner from Auntie Joan with Mum and Vince. Mum's neck is covered in love bites. This must stop. I don't think Vince can believe his luck. Six weeks ago he didn't even have a mouldy sandwich to chew on.

MONDAY, MARCH 1ST
A new month and a new start. I don't have many clothes but they're all packed and I'm ready to go. Auntie Joan has made me a sandwich and has given me three pounds. Mum has paid for the train fare to Manchester and Vince has got out of bed to see me off. I arrive at five and will find a taxi that hopefully will take me to the digs.

TUESDAY, MARCH 2ND

The digs are ok and in bed now very tired. I rehearsed all day with Tom and Jen, my fellow actors. They are really good and I have to be good myself to keep up with them. The rest of the team are Bob who seems to do everything, and Alf who walks with a comedy limp and seems to do nothing. Anne is the director and is in charge. She looks a bit like Diana Dors only not as pretty or as blonde so nothing like her really.

WEDNESDAY, MARCH 3RD

Early finish today as we all went to see Ralph McTell in concert tonight. I'm the youngest but they all seem a good bunch and I think that they're all trying to look after me a bit. The concert seemed to be full of hippies who could all do with a good wash. I've never heard of folk music and it was a bit boring. Alf didn't go. He stayed in the pub to play darts saying, 'that he didn't want to hear some long-haired Herbert whining'. I think that he'd get on well with Auntie Joan.

THURSDAY, MARCH 4TH

I rang Susan's work this morning and whoever answered said she wasn't around to take my call. They were lying. I could hear her in the background probably talking to Paul McCartney. This play is full of anger and emotions and I hope the people in the clubs that we are touring can understand it. I'm buggered if I can. On the walk back to the digs we saw a massive fight between skinheads and some Indian blokes. We hid in a shop doorway until the police came and broke it up. Alf said that 'a spot of National Service would sort the lot of them out'. Only two more days of rehearsals left and then we hit the road. Our first performance is on Sunday afternoon. I've no idea if we will be ready in time.

FRIDAY, MARCH 5TH

Rehearsed again all day today and then we went for a quick drink afterwards. It looks like Anne is keen on Bob our 'everything man 'as he is known. I stayed in the pub until Alf starting talking about the war and how he hates the 'fucking Bosch'. On the way back to the digs I kept an eye out for stray skinheads. Jen has a mate who's playing in a group tomorrow so we're all going to see them.

SATURDAY, MARCH 6TH

Our final dress rehearsal today while Bob and Alf were checking out the first club for tomorrow's show. Rehearsal went well and it looks like it's all finally come together, apart from a couple of fluffed lines and missing marks. We met Bob at the pub where Jen's band were playing. They were called The Sweet and they were dead good but very noisy. Alf arrived, ordered a pint of bitter and then walked straight out again once the group had started. Jen said the band were on the verge of getting a big recording contract. I'm not so sure about that.

SUNDAY, MARCH 7TH

Today was show day and it went ok. I made a couple of mistakes, once when my character was having an emotional speech I forgot Tom's name and called him Bob and I knocked over a chair on my way to the other side of the stage, but I think the audience of about twenty five thought it was all part of the play. Anne seemed to be pleased though and she didn't have to do any shouting. She said that there wasn't many in this afternoon as most of Manchester were probably at home watching *The Golden Shot*.

MONDAY, MARCH 8TH

I slept in this morning and I missed the greasy bacon sandwich served up by Mrs Dunne, our landlady. I packed my bag and on the way to the club I bought a chicken pie and a Kit Kat. We rehearsed again before the show and it went a lot better this evening. Only about thirty people in tonight. Are they repeating *The Golden Shot*? Tomorrow we all head off to Stockport, wherever that is.

TUESDAY, MARCH 9TH

Alf arrived in the transit van at eleven o'clock and we all piled in the back among the lights and various bits of scenery. Being the youngest I ended up on the floor. Jen and Tom sat on a bench seat which moved from side to side when we took a corner too fast. Anne was up front snuggling up to Bob who was next to a farting, coughing, driving Alf. It wasn't that long a journey. Jen played Mungo Jerry on her cassette while Tom and me swapped over reading between *The Beano* and the *NME*. We stopped at the motorway services so Alf could have a slash and moan about being the 'only fucking driver'. We got to the new digs around mid- afternoon. It looks a bit like the house that *The Addams Family* live in, only older.

WEDNESDAY, MARCH 10TH

So now we all know now, Anne and Bob are definitely 'at it'. They are both in a double room. I'm sharing with Tom and Jen's got a single. Alf's got his own room because nobody in their right mind would share with a moaning, miserable old git like him. We set up this morning and had a really quick run through ready for the show tonight.

THURSDAY, MARCH 11TH

There were over fifty people in tonight and most of them pissed themselves laughing when the back wall to the basement fell down mid-performance. Luckily, I was off stage and along with Anne we managed to pick it up and prop it back up until the interval. At the time of the disaster Alf was in the toilet having a crap. Bob and Anne celebrated our 'success' tonight by having very noisy rampant sex which all of us and half of Stockport could hear.

FRIDAY, MARCH 12TH

I missed breakfast this morning while still dreaming of that bloody wall falling down. Jen, Tom and me later went for lunch in Daniels while Bob, Anne and Alf went to fix the scenery. Most of the talk between us was what a noisy cow Anne is and what would Bob's wife do if she could hear them. We spent the afternoon playing Cluedo and Scrabble, and I don't care what they say 'Lycton' is a word and I'm not stupid! The performance tonight was much better and everything stayed upright especially Bob later as we all heard again.

SATURDAY, MARCH 13TH

An early start this morning as we are off to Oldham. Alf constantly bored the shit out of us by telling an unfunny joke about old hams going to Oldham. When we stopped for food and a wee I found a phone booth and tried to call Susan. Her dim-witted brother answered and said she's shopping at Wembley Market. That's a lie. Wembley Market only opens on Sundays. I expect that I'm going to get dumped again soon. Arrived early afternoon when most of Oldham was already closed.

SUNDAY, MARCH 14TH

This working men's club in Oldham is such a dump. Alf says it's because of the bomb damage caused by the dirty Bosch during the war. There's a plaque outside the club's toilets that says, 'This club was opened by the Mayor of Oldham in 1959', but that doesn't seem to bother Alf.

MONDAY, MARCH 15TH

I rang Auntie Joan this morning and I got well told off for not ringing sooner. She's right of course. Mum is still with Vince and they are talking about joining the Sally Army, I don't think the Sally Army are that desperate. Jen's boyfriend Bernie arrives tonight, so no doubt we will have noisy sex ringing out all over the North of England in stereo tonight.

TUESDAY, MARCH 16TH

Our performance last night was truly terrible and the locals had every right to run us out of town. Luckily, they only chose not to applaud at the end although quite a few had already left by then. We all missed a load of cues, and Tom had a nightmare forgetting his lines. At one stage I had a conversation with myself for about thirty seconds. Anne gave us a right bollocking, and we deserved it. This morning the only sound anyone could hear at the breakfast table was Alf murdering a full English with lots of French mustard.

WEDNESDAY, MARCH 17TH

There's no show tonight so we walked around Stalybridge to see what was happening on St Patrick's Night. The answer was not a lot but we did find a pub and inside were a few Irish blokes who were building something somewhere. A big Orange one called Kevin was starting to show a bit too much interest in Anne so Bob slipped a few gins into his pints of Guinness and he was soon unconscious.

THURSDAY, MARCH 18TH

The performance tonight was much better and the audience actually seemed to enjoy it. It's such a pity that there were only about twenty-five people there. Alf is really starting to get on everyone's nerves at the moment. He won't stop blooding moaning. The latest is that he thinks he might have a spasticated back from doing too much driving. What the fuck is a spasticated back and if there is such a thing Bob says it's only a matter of time before he blames it on the Germans. Anne also tried to tell him that if he has got a bad back, then it's almost certainly because he fell over a garden wall walking back to the digs last week when he'd had too many pints of bitter.

FRIDAY, MARCH 19TH

I 'checked in' with Auntie Joan this morning and I wished I hadn't bothered. Mum and Vince are getting engaged. Auntie Joan wants to know where I'll be on Monday as it's my birthday and she wants to send me a card. I said thanks but don't worry as my birthday is not until April! I think she might be going a bit funny. Tonight's show was the best yet and most of the crowd stayed until the end and didn't go to the bar. Tomorrow we are off to Glossop, if such a place really exists.

SATURDAY, MARCH 20TH

This morning in a transport café I watched Bob standing behind Alf and he had a knife clutched firmly in his hand. I thought for a second that possibly he was preparing to plunge it into the back of Alf's nut but no, he was getting it so Anne could eat her eggburger. For some reason Alf has now got a thing about Ken Dodd saying at numerous times what an ugly, unfunny fucker he is, and how when he worked with him once he stole his jokes. He even said yesterday 'those little bastard diddymen were my idea'. We set up quickly this afternoon for tonight's show and Bob still has the knife.

SUNDAY, MARCH 21ST

A quick head count last night through the curtains showed that there were only sixteen people watching. Surely that won't even pay for the cost of the digs and petrol. Anne's always positive but even she seems a bit low at the moment. We even think the shagging with Bob has slacked off a bit because we haven't heard anything for ages. At least there's more room in the van now that Jen's boyfriend has gone home. A Sunday off today spent mostly sleeping and thinking of girls, any girl.

MONDAY, MARCH 22ND

Travelling to Wilmslow this morning which the wisely Alf tells us is full of 'rich, lazy wankers'. We stopped at a café and I treated myself to a can of Tab and a walnut whip. Jen says she's missing Bernie already. I'm not sure she's cut out for touring. I don't mind it, I haven't really got anyone to miss me that much as I'm convinced Susan's already dumped me but has just forgotten to tell me.

TUESDAY, MARCH 23RD

For once Alf might just be right, Wilmslow British Legion club is posh and the people were lovely. After we had set up we found our new digs and met our landlady, Mrs Hawkins and her daughter Grace. Grace looked about my age and she's drop dead gorgeous. Her tits looked so luscious that you could eat your dinner off them. I fancy her like crazy and I'm going to try and do something about it.

WEDNESDAY, MARCH 24TH

Well I've just spent the night in between the silky thighs of an eighteen-year-old goddess. Well, that's not strictly true. During the interval Grace came backstage to tell me to meet her at the bottom of her garden because she wanted me to 'shag service' her in the potting shed. It wasn't exactly Romeo and Juliet in fact at one stage as I was going at it with her, I saw a fox having a shit in the garden, but in its own way sex in a moonlight shed sounds quite romantic. Apparently, she enjoyed it so much that I'm going to get an encore tomorrow night, so I need to go out and find a chemist for some French letters and possibly a torch. It will be nice to see what I'm getting.

THURSDAY, MARCH 25TH

I spent most of today thinking about Dirty Grace. She's been at college all day. I should really be thinking about my performance on stage tonight and not in the potting shed later. I don't feel the least bit guilty about Grace, even Mary Whitehouse must have a bit as her birthday gets nearer. When we left for the show earlier I got a nasty look from Grace's mum. I reckon that potting shed gets used a fair bit. Perhaps I might not be saying Grace tonight after all.

FRIDAY, MARCH 26TH

A really good show last night. It's just a pity that as we are coming towards the end of the run we are getting really good. The potting shed was indeed busy again, that girl has got some energy and thankfully very low morals, just like me.

SATURDAY, MARCH 27TH

As we pulled out of Wilmslow in the van this morning my fellow actor 'bastards' gave a hearty rendition of *Amazing Grace,* evidently everyone was watching us perform while they tucked into their Ovaltines. Alf was so disgusted with me that he didn't talk to me all day long, so that was one positive. Back in Manchester now and we are booked in to a decent hotel at last. We finally all have our own rooms although everyone on our floor has to share the bathroom which believe me is not a nice experience if you're going in after Alf. On a walk through Manchester I noticed that *Please Sir* was showing at the local cinema, so turning down the offer of lunch I decided to go and see myself on the big screen. I did see myself, only for a few seconds but it made me dead happy and a little bit proud of myself for once.

SUNDAY, MARCH 28TH

Most of this morning was spent fighting for the bathroom with Jen and Tom. At lunch in the pub Anne and Bob looked all loved up again. Perhaps it's because that they have to go back to their normal lives soon like the rest of us. Alf was quick to remind everyone that 'in my day married couples stayed married and you kept your tackle fastened in your trousers'. I thought Bob was definitely going to stab him this time. Thank God the Arctic Roll and Angel Delight arrived, it calmed everyone down.

MONDAY, MARCH 29TH

Again it seems that Anne was right. Last night the place was packed and they all seemed to be enjoying the play. We actually took three curtain calls and the mood back stage was the best it's ever been. Later, Anne called me a little genius but I think that had more to do with her being pissed on gin. During the celebrations I stupidly rang and woke up Auntie Joan to remind her that I would be home on Wednesday. She joked that she'd already let out my room to the postman called Ali. At least I hope that she was joking, she's always had this thing about Indian men in uniforms.

TUESDAY, MARCH 30TH

Not such a big audience tonight but everything went well again and again they all seemed to like it. We are all heading home tomorrow but not before we all have breakfast together. There might possibly be last night sex for Anne and Bob before he goes back to his wife.

WEDNESDAY, MARCH 31ST

A weird and sad day really. Going home to a slightly nutty auntie and the lady and the tramp. It's nearly time to say my goodbyes and ride off into the sunset as my new found friends shout 'Shane, Shane, come back Shane'.

THURSDAY, APRIL 1ST

A strange feeling this morning when I woke up. I realised it's April Fool's Day and I'm back home. I wasn't very clever at school but don't they call that irony or something. It's also my birthday. There's obviously a handwritten letter from Susan waiting for me to open. I'm not opening it yet. I've got a card and presents from Auntie Joan to open first. Auntie Joan has knitted me a jumper with the word Actor on it. She must have worked hard knitting that but there's not a fucking chance in hell of me ever wearing it. I'd look like one of the silly boys on the school special bus. The lady and the tramp have bought me a card and a bottle of Brut aftershave and a jigsaw of the Tower of London. I can only dream of what goes on in my Mum's head. I've decided not to read the letter from Susan yet, there's no point, I know what's in it.

FRIDAY, APRIL 2ND

So, curiosity got the better of me and I read the letter. Susan and her dad have finished with me once and for all, but Lucien seems to love me. He has rung this morning to offer me the radio workshop thing that I thought was dead and gone. He said that everybody was saying good things about me and that more work was sure to follow. He also said that there was a postal order for nineteen pounds in the post which I should get tomorrow. I went for a walk later and had a samosa and chips for dinner and I bought a *Southall Gazette* to check what was on at the pictures this week end. I saw that the small mucky cinema in Ealing is showing *Percy*. I knew this would happen. By this time tomorrow my bare arse will be on show to everyone in West London who wants to pay to see it.

SATURDAY, APRIL 3RD

Weirdly, I thought of going to Southall Market this morning and buying a false beard and dark glasses so I could go and see *Percy* this afternoon, but after a quick think I know I would just end up looking like somebody my Mum would fancy who was watching a dirty film. I met Tommy Smith later and I got talked into going to Cheekee Pete's disco in Richmond tonight. God knows how much this is going to cost.

SUNDAY, APRIL 4TH

I got so drunk last night that I can't remember getting home. I must face facts and realise that I'm just not a drinker. I've stayed upstairs most of the day because I think I was sick somewhere when I came in although I just don't remember where. It's five in the afternoon and I must go down and face Auntie Joan soon. Back to bed now and it seems I was sick all over Auntie Joan's daffs in the front garden. I'll buy her some more tomorrow. I've also found a scrap of paper with a phone number on it. It says 'love Alex' with a great big kiss. I hope Alex is a girl.

TUESDAY, APRIL 6TH

I have a bit of money so I went to Woolworth's and bought *Hot Love* by the singer who looks like a long haired pixie. I don't know his name. I played it until Auntie Joan got fed up and started swearing. To say sorry for the being sick incident I bought Auntie Joan a box of Milk Tray. When she opened them all the coffee creams were missing and she started swearing again.

WEDNESDAY, APRIL 7TH

We have a new postman who Auntie Joan calls Punjab Pat and he delivered a large envelope for me it's from Lucien. The radio play script is *Julius Caesar* and I'm playing the part of Brutus. There's tons to learn. He also sent some copies of reviews that Anne had sent him and they said good things about me having stage presence and generally nice things. I went through the script properly tonight and this Brutus character talks a lot and seems to be a right pain in the arse.

THURSDAY APRIL 8TH.

The little pixie was on *Top of the Pops* tonight singing *Hot Love* and I think I'm beginning to fancy him. Am I turning into a bum boy?

FRIDAY, APRIL 9TH

I've had 'dirty' Barbara and 'amazing' Grace but I can't seem to get Susan out of my head. I know she doesn't want me again but why am I still thinking about her and the cemetery. Mum and Vince called in tonight and Mum said that she wants to marry Vince. I thought Auntie Joan was going to have a heart attack, even Vince looked surprised. It's Easter but nobody bothers with eggs in this family.

SATURDAY, APRIL 10TH

A very surprising and not unpleasant day today. This morning while walking around Southall Market a girl asked me out. I must be irresistible. Her name is Shirley and she was buying a lipstick and a Crunchie from spotty Brian's stall. She looks like a bit of a hippy but she has enormous tits and nice lips. Tonight, we are meeting in the White Hart pub and then getting the bus to Ealing to see a group she knows called Edison Lighthouse.

SUNDAY, APRIL 11TH

Shirley's all right and she knows tons about music and art. She loves it that I'm an actor although I might have exaggerated my acting experience a bit. She does have a lot of weird friends though who seem to be so drugged up on joints that they talked more bullshit than mum. After a quick snog on those lovely lips we agreed to meet again on Wednesday. I like this one.

MONDAY, APRIL 12TH

This Julius Caesar part is really hard. I'm thinking of ringing Lucien and saying that I might be a bit out of my depth here with this. Auntie Joan has had a bit of a fall, but she won't go to the doctor. She says her friend Minnie told her that our new doctor used to be a vet in Calcutta, so she says 'he's not fucking telling me that I've got distemper'. She should know better but I think Auntie Joan is turning into someone who doesn't like foreigners. She's a batty old woman.

TUESDAY, APRIL 13TH

This morning I had a bit of an argument with Auntie Joan. She says that I use her phone too much and after a bit of a row I had to admit that she's probably right. The crafty old woman had kept a list of all my calls since I've been back, so I really didn't have much to say after that. We agreed that I would give her another one pound fifty a week and she was happy with that as it means she can go to bingo on Thursdays now. I rang Lucien this morning and told him I was struggling with learning this *Julius Caesar* play. I got a bit annoyed when I heard him laughing down the phone. He said that I was a silly boy and that had I forgotten that when actors work on the radio there are no cameras so I can read the lines on the script when I speak them. I told him that I didn't forget, and as I've never worked on the radio before how the hell would I know that. He gave me a great, big, loud smoochy kiss down the phone and told me not to be so silly. I think Lucien would get on well with that T-Rex fella.

WEDNESDAY, APRIL 14TH

I stood for ages outside the White Hart waiting for Shirley but she didn't turn up. This hasn't happened to me before and I don't like it. Just to make my mood worse I bumped into Anthony and Peggy in the Wimpy and they are getting engaged. I am happy for them though and we are going to go out together soon.

THURSDAY, APRIL 15TH

Even though I could read the script I still took some time to try to learn it, I had nothing else to do. I later watched *Crossroads* and then a film called *Beneath the Twelve Mile Reef.* Both were awful. The actors in *Crossroads* could have done with reading their lines instead of trying to remember them. A bit of the scenery shook so much when the dim-witted Benny closed a door, I thought the whole wall was going to fall down on top of him and his bobble hat. Auntie Joan was at bingo so I had a Kit Kat, Toffee Crisp and a packet of Rolos for my tea. Tomorrow morning I will wake up looking like Spotty Muldoon.

FRIDAY, APRIL 16TH

Another boring day so I went for a walk around Woolworth's thinking that I might see Shirley and her lips. I noticed one or two of the women who work there watching me closely. I'm certain that they think that I'm some sort of trainee shoplifter, so I brought a packet of bunion plasters for twenty five pence. I'm not even sure that I know what a fucking bunion is.

SATURDAY, APRIL 17TH

I don't really like football, but this afternoon to get away from Auntie Joan I walked over to the rec and watched two teams playing each other. A team in blue spent ten minutes trying to kick a team dressed in white without too much success. When someone booted the ball into the canal I decided to go home, thinking was all that really worth getting all dressed up for?

SUNDAY, APRIL 18TH

I met Anthony and Peggy last night and they had a surprise for me. Peggy's cousin Bridget is visiting from Ireland and they sort of set us up on a blind date. Bridget was so skinny that if she turned sideways and poked her tongue out she'd look like a zip. She's got a real strong Irish accent but is decent looking enough in a country girl sort of way. We all went to Samantha's disco in Ealing and we had a bit of a snog during a slow song by the Carpenters. It didn't go any further though because I'm sure Peggy must have told her that I had very low morals and was only after a quick shag. Still, Bridget was nice and she was a cheap date being a skinny bird. She didn't eat or drink much which is surprising for an Irish girl.

MONDAY, APRIL 19TH
Brilliant, a cheque arrived this morning for eighteen pounds and fifty pence. This was the final payment for the *Basement* tour. I gave Auntie Joan five pounds so tonight she cooked boil in the bag fish and Birds Eye peas for my tea, followed by Arctic roll and condensed milk for pudding.

TUESDAY, APRIL 20TH
I thought of seeing Peggy at lunchtime today with a view of having another go at Bridget but I must stop acting like a dirty old tom cat or even my mum. Read through the play again this afternoon and I know my part now even though I don't necessarily understand it.

WEDNESDAY, APRIL 21ST
I watched *On the Buses* again tonight. I nearly killed myself.

THURSDAY, APRIL 22ND
Bored, Shakespeare. Bored, Shakespeare. No girlfriend. No life. No hope.

FRIDAY, APRIL 23RD

Shit, the Classic cinema in Hayes is now showing *Percy* late on Saturday night, it will be full of dirty old men in dirty old raincoats who have all probably 'known' my Mum. I shouldn't have done that film.

SATURDAY, APRIL 24TH

From the result of my good reviews from the Basement tour I received a letter from Lucien about some possible telly work. It's one day's work next Friday on something called *For the Love of Ada*. After the radio play on Monday and Tuesday I've got to go and see Lucien for details. I watched something new tonight. It was called *Candid Camera* and was dead funny.

SUNDAY, APRIL 25TH

A peace offering from Auntie Joan today to mum and Vince. They are coming here for Sunday dinner. Mum now has pink hair from a perm by Crusty Alice that went wrong under the drier. Vince is now starting to look a bit like that Greek bloke who's married to the Queen, he's called Philip I think. We never did history at school because Mr Daniels, the history teacher, ran off to Gretna Green with a girl who worked at Mac Fisheries. There was a rumour going around Southall that Mr Daniels ended up in Wormwood Scrubs in a special wing built only for nonces and gypsies. Mum has certainly changed a bit. She says she now listens to *Mrs Dale's Diary* and she had even baked a cake for pudding. We all said it tasted lovely but it was horrendous.

MONDAY, APRIL 26TH

It's ten o'clock and I'm home after a long day at the BBC Maida Vale studios. After nervously reporting to Jean in the reception I was led into the studio to meet the others and start the recording, and I really enjoyed it. I actually managed to read out all the right things at all the right times. At lunch in the canteen a girl recognised me from the *Please Sir* film shoot. She asked me why I was only on the filming for a couple of days and I told her that I had to leave because I was touring in a Pinter play. Total bullshit of course, but it sounded good to say it. Went to sleep feeling very happy and looking forward to tomorrow's recording, like a proper actor would.

TUESDAY, APRIL 27TH

It's a wrap, all finished and off I went to the pub with my fellow actors talking nonsense about acting and things. Tonight while writing this, I'm back in my tiny bedroom living with my batty auntie and back to reality.

WEDNESDAY, APRIL 28TH

So Auntie Joan tells me this morning that she's now got a boyfriend. She met Amit in a queue while she was waiting to buy some new surgical stockings from a stall on Southall Market. He's apparently a Hindu but she says that didn't put her off him one bit. It seems everybody in my family is now getting a bit except me. This afternoon I met Lucien at his office and he had good news for me. I have got a small part in that television programme called *For the love of Ada*. I only have one line so I won't be sent a script. My day for filming will be on Monday and I am to go to Teddington studios for nine in the morning and then be taken to Teddington cemetery for the filming. On the way home I thought of the last time that I was in a cemetery with Susan and I quickly had to think of Giant Haystacks to make my old fella go down before I got off the train.

THURSDAY, APRIL 29TH

I love acting while I'm doing it but it's the time in between I can't stand. So bored today that I went shopping with mum who wanted to buy a dress for the first time in years. Vince went to see Bob Walker, the barber, to get his hair cut and hopefully make him look a bit less like that Greek fella and more like Tony Curtis. Auntie Joan thought she'd do something nice for Amit so she made him a spicy curry, but when he came to see her tonight he asked her what that awful stinky smell coming from the kitchen was. He doesn't like curries and was looking forward to bangers and mash for dinner. She sulked until he went home.

FRIDAY, APRIL 30TH

I looked in the A to Z today to see where Teddington was. It's bleeding miles away from Southall and could well take me at least a week to get there. While walking through the King Street today I was sure I saw that Shirley bird who stood me up. I only saw her from behind but I'm certain it was her, a shame because she looked great and has a lovely bum. I've decided that it doesn't matter what's on I'm going to the pictures tomorrow.

SATURDAY, MAY 1ST

This afternoon I went to Ealing where they were showing *Dad's Army* the film, not the telly programme. It was all the same actors and like the telly programme funny for a while until it gets on your nerves a bit. I was feeling a bit sorry for myself being on my own when on the way out I bumped into a girl who I used to go to school with. Her name is Debra and she was with her cousin who had a patch over one eye called Sandra, the cousin was called Sandra not her patch. Debra wrote her phone number down on the back of an empty Bar Six wrapper. I will definitely call her. I always fancied her at school but I always thought that she didn't like naughty dark boys.

SUNDAY, MAY 2ND

I didn't waste any time this morning so I rang Debra. We are going out on Wednesday night, don't know where yet. Auntie Joan has taught Amit the rules for bingo. I didn't know there were any rules. I thought it was just a load of old people listening out for a number and then crossing it off on a card. If you're lucky you get all the numbers crossed out and you win a bottle of shitty wine or some mouldy old meat. I had a bath tonight. Tomorrow I catch two trains and two buses to Teddington Studios. I will get up at six.

MONDAY, MAY 3RD

I think it would be fair to say that that wasn't the best day I've had since I started acting. *For the Love of Ada* is about an old couple who live in a house in a cemetery. They are so old in real life that's it's surely only a matter of time before they are both lying in the cemetery for good. The main male actor is Wilfred Pickles and he didn't talk to anyone all day, although I did once hear him say 'who's the darkie lad?' to the director. Old Wilfred played a gravedigger who shouts at a boy who was supposedly stealing some flowers from a grave. The boy had to shout back 'mind your own business,' to our hero as he ran away. Yes, I was that boy and yes, I remembered my line. I then went back and sat on the studio bus. I'm going to get six pounds and fifty pence for today and it cost me one pound and seventy- five pence to get here and then go home. I brought a saveloy and chips on the way back along with two pickled onions and a big bottle of Coke, so I'm nearly out of pocket now. I'm certain Kenny Lynch never started out like this.

TUESDAY, MAY 4TH
Bored, watching boring old school programmes. I now know why I never took any notice of them when I was at school.

WEDNESDAY, MAY 5TH
Why do weird things always happen to me? When I rang Debra last night we agreed to meet in the White Swan pub at seven o'clock. With Auntie Joan out again at bingo my plan was to get Debra quickly tipsy with a view to getting her on Auntie Joan's settee by about half past eight, bra-less and panting, and her telling me how much she'd always loved me. I arrived at the pub at ten to seven and wasn't that pleased that Tommy Smith and his workmates from the laundry had popped in

for a quick pint on the way home. I told Tommy that I was meeting Debra Findley for hopefully a night of shagging before my auntie got back with Amit from the bingo. Tommy said his mate Barry had been out with Debra and she was a right raver who liked dressing up and kinky stuff. At exactly seven o'clock the pub doors opened and the lovely Debra walked in dressed as a fucking Salvation Army girl and she was there with her Lieutenant called Arnold who started to try and flog copies of *The Watchtower* to Tommy and his mates who by now were in fucking hysterics. Why didn't she tell me she was religious when she gave me her number when we met at the cinema? She said she'd been a soldier of Jesus for about a year now and that she could tell I needed saving when she saw me on Saturday. I said thanks and then went for a piss and climbed out of the back window in the cubicle and walked home quickly.

FRIDAY, MAY 7TH

I'm staying in for a few days at the moment. I won't be going in any pubs or churches. *The Dick Emery Show* was on tonight. He's funny. One of his old women characters definitely looks like my mum.

SATURDAY, MAY 8TH

Evidently, the BBC say it's Cup Final day with Arsenal playing Liverpool. It's at Wembley where the market is. Why is it on all day on both channels?

SUNDAY, MAY 9TH

I will ring Lucien in the morning. I was lying in bed last night thinking about when I was on tour. I was happy and I want to do it again.

MONDAY, MAY 10TH

I rang Ace academy and Lucien is away on holiday but Mindy, his assistant, took my call and heard my moans. She said she will get back to me this week, I won't hear anymore from her again. Mum and Vince called round tonight and asked Auntie Joan if she wanted to take over the rental of the massive telly that they have got. Auntie Joan said: 'Don't be stupid, I'm not the Queen of Sheba.' For once I felt sorry for mum. She said she and Vince didn't watch much telly now and she was only trying to be nice. I wasn't interested but Vince told me that Arsenal won the football match at Wembley on Saturday with a goal by Charlie George, but he might have said George Charlie.

FRIDAY, MAY 14TH

So, after days of boring telly and endless spam sandwiches for dinner, today I finally heard from Mindy, just like I knew I would. I have the offer of a job at the Liverpool Empire in a play called *Home and Beauty* written by Somerset Maugham whose name is nearly as silly as George Charlie. Rehearsals start next Thursday and we open in three weeks. I played 'hard to get' and said yes straight away without even asking about the money and for any details of the part and for how long the play was going to run for. I'm such a twerp.

SATURDAY, MAY 15TH

I did a potentially stupid thing today but I've been in the house for so long I just had to get out. I went to the cinema in Ealing tonight to see *Soldier Blue*, hoping that I wouldn't bump into Sally Army Debra again. I can honestly say that Debra wouldn't have been anywhere near this film. It was violent and horrible and I didn't like it at all. I should have gone next door and watched *Dad's Army* again.

SUNDAY, MAY 16TH

The *News of the World* said this morning that Kenny Lynch is going out with a model girl called Patsy, the lucky bastard. *The Golden Shot* was on again this afternoon, still unbelievably nobody killed yet. I did walk up to Mr Patel's on the corner and I bought myself a Fray Bentos pie and a Crunchie for tea. Auntie Joan had gone to Amit's for a curry. Something I wouldn't have believed two months ago, he's having egg and chips.

MONDAY, MAY 17TH

A large envelope came through the letter box today addressed Dessie Twelvetrees Esq. It was all my details plus the script for the play in Liverpool. I think it is fair to say that after a quick flick through I shouldn't have any problem learning my lines. I've only got ten. I am playing Clarence, an errand boy, who seems a bit of a half- wit, so I should be ideal for the role. The whole cast meets on Thursday in a Scout hut near the theatre to start rehearsals. The digs are on Lime street which is near the theatre. I haven't told Auntie Joan yet, although I don't think that she will be too upset now Amit's on the scene, and mum won't even miss me until she wants some fags from Mr Patel's.

TUESDAY, MAY 18TH

I had to ring Ace this morning because after reading the details of the play there's still no mention of money or how long the run is. Lucien who's back from Cornwall told me the run is for two weeks at twenty pounds a week. There's an option of another week at the end but evidently that all depends on whether the 'scousers' understand the comedy of Somerset Maugham, which I thought was a bit rude but then I don't know any 'scousers'. I leave tomorrow and I've just realised that all my underpants are dirty and that I don't know how to get to Liverpool!

WEDNESDAY, MAY 19TH

I have arrived at my digs and I have already met two of my fellow actors. Sisters Sally and Angela Tongs are sharing a room and a bathroom just down the corridor from me, and it seems, like me, that they are already shit scared of our landlady. Mrs Hughes is a woman who seems to be the size of a small hippo that has a permanent toothache and very bad breath. All three of us arrived roughly at the same time this afternoon and old hippo breath made us sign a sort of contract that said, no shagging, no drinking, no smoking and be in by eleven thirty otherwise you sleep in the garden. At the bottom of the contract it read, Welcome to the Shangri La. On the way down on the train this morning I read the script again and went over my lines. This seems like a funny play and I already know my lines I hope, but tomorrow we shall find out.

THURSDAY, MAY 20TH

Today has been a very long but pretty good day. We are rehearsing in a Scout hut until next Thursday when we then move to the theatre. The hut has quickly been christened Mrs Hughes because it is big and smelly and one of the storerooms is full of crap. This was the girl's idea not mine. The other actors are evidently in the much more luxurious Sandy Banks Hotel complete with indoor swimming pool and cocktail lounge. We have a cast of eleven plus a nice man called John Elms who seems to be the director although I fear clashes already with the leading lady Bunty Swoon who is the producer and the general bigwig, as she once played a ward sister in *Emergency Ward Ten* back in the late Sixties. The two leading men Charles and the strangely named Gideon seem like good sorts and are hinting about getting me and the girls drunk and then dumping us on Mrs Hughes's doorstep and ringing the bell and running away like two frightened schoolgirls. Bunty didn't talk to me or the girls today. Gideon joked it's because we are too far down the cast list and she doesn't want to waste her breath on what she calls underlings. I think he's right but it's early days yet.

FRIDAY, MAY 21ST

All the actors here are really good and although I'm not that experienced I can already tell that this play will be dead good. In a way I'm glad that I've only got a small part. I will be okay playing a half -wit errand boy, my old teachers at Featherstone School would say that I was made for the part. After rehearsals everybody except Bunty and Bette who plays the cook, went for a drink and something to eat in a pub just near the theatre. I only had a Coke and a cheese roll but most of them got rat arsed on brandy and barley wine. Sally and Angela don't drink at all so I don't think I'm going to have much luck with them at all. We got back at nine o'clock so well within curfew.

SATURDAY, MAY 22ND

It might be the weekend but the cast of *Home and Beauty* work on. Before rehearsals at nine thirty this morning I rang Auntie Joan and Amit answered the phone. Now whatever way this works out I've got a problem with him being there this morning. If Auntie Joan says he's staying in her bed at nights now, even though it's got nothing to do with me and I've got the morals of an alley cat, should seventy-year-olds really be doing it? On the other hand if she says that he's sleeping in the spare bedroom, then the bugger's sleeping in my bed while I'm away. Anyway, I asked Auntie Joan, and she said: 'Mind your own fucking business, boy', so I suppose I deserved that. Bunty spoke to me today. She said, 'not bad', just two words but at least she noticed the darkly skinned boy. I think Angela is starting to flirt with me which is a bit of a worry because she's the uglier sister and Sally, the dead pretty one, is the one that I want.

SUNDAY, MAY 23RD

A big lie in this morning and then a sausage sandwich and two cups of tea in the café with the girls before work again this afternoon. This evening the whole cast went for a drink in the bar of the Sandy Banks Hotel. Only Gideon and Samantha who plays Mrs Shuttleworth sat with the three stooges which is what Gideon has now nicknamed us. On the walk back both Angela and Sally held my hand. I might end up having to service them both.

MONDAY, MAY 24TH

Bunty went into a massive temper with Gideon who turned up pissed this morning with a mighty hangover. To make matters worse, on his entrance into the bedroom in Act One this morning, he spewed up and the whole mess hit the floor and bounced onto Bunty's shoes as she was in mid-speech. When the rest of us had stopped laughing we noticed that Bunty had slipped over as she attempted to run away and had landed face down with her head very nearly settled in the bedroom waste paper bin. Gideon tried to help her up but she told him to 'fuck off and die somewhere', which was surprising language for someone who's starred in *Emergency Ward Ten*. Some of us are off tomorrow night to see a group called The Scaffold who have had lots of hits but of course I've never heard of them. Tomorrow night might also be the night when I have a bash at Sally. I'm getting randy.

WEDNESDAY, MAY 26TH

It's been an incredible couple of days and it's probably not going to slow down any. On the work front Bunty is only talking to Gideon through her character Victoria. When she's Bunty he can still 'fuck off and die'. The rest of us think that it is hilarious including Gideon who is playing up to the whole thing brilliantly. Director John couldn't care less and as long as he's in the bar at the hotel by six every night then he's happy. My intentions to make love to Sally worked like a dream on Tuesday. It was as we were both going at it like Bugs Bunny and his horny rabbit girlfriend that things took a surprising twist. As I was just taking Sally past the finishing line, naked sister number two climbed aboard and joined the ride. After a brief nod and a whisper from Sally of 'we share everything,' I stumbled into teenage boy heaven. I am in my own bed now and I'm well and truly knackered. Sally and Angela may be a couple of years older than me but blimey northern girls really have got some energy.

THURSDAY, MAY 27TH

I thought at breakfast this morning that the mood over the cornflakes might be a little awkward, but the girls are just the same bubbly blondes that they usually are. I'm pretty sure old dragon breath Mrs Hughes knows something filthy went on last night but surprisingly there wasn't a lot of noise around considering a mini-orgy was taking place in one of her bedrooms. This morning we are rehearsing at the theatre for the first time complete with scenery and stage clothes. Today went ok, the Liverpool Empire is massive and has thousands of seats, well, probably hundreds but it's still massive. The scenery guys are brilliant and a good laugh. They can change the scenery around really quickly once the curtain has come down. We open on Saturday night and I heard Bunty tell John that over two hundred tickets have been sold. She also told him that it must be because quite a few have booked to see Sister Pauline from the telly. She's such a fucking big head, for all she knows they might have come to see that half caste lad from that mucky film *Percy*. Angela knocked on the door earlier and we had a quick one which was handy because I was half way through a Topic when she knocked and it was beginning to melt.

FRIDAY, MAY 28TH

This acting lark really is very easy. I would love to make up some more lines for me but I think Bunty would kill me if I did. Angela and Sally keep swapping roles deliberately but nobody seems to care as long as a serving girl comes on stage at the right time at the right place. Gideon says that for Bunty the three of us are just cannon fodder to make her look good. I might bring her out the wrong prop accidentally on purpose on the last night and then we will see how 'Scary Poppins' as everyone now calls her, handles it. Angela visited tonight because she says she's got women's problems coming at the weekend. I'm pretty sure I know what she means. I just love these dirty northern girls.

SATURDAY, MAY 29TH

Up early this morning so I rang Auntie Joan and once again Amit was there. He's obviously staying overnight now. It seems everyone in my family are sex mad, but seventy-year-olds doing it doesn't bear thinking about. Mum and Vince are organising a jumble sale this morning for the homeless tramps of Middlesex so Vince should get a new suit and some shoes. A group called Middle of the Road are in a record shop in town this morning advertising their new single, so Sally and me are going to have a look. Angela's still in bed, not well and for once alone. When we got to the record shop there were only about ten people who had bothered to show up. The record is called *Chirpy Chirpy Cheep Cheep*, so we were not surprised that the shop was nearly empty. Sally's nice and a lot calmer than her noisy sister. She told me that they started acting after they left a children's home that they were put in after their mum had died. Their dad had walked out and left them just after Angela was born. I told her that my dad walked out just after I was made. Sally said that my mum should tell me who he is so that I could track him down and get to know him. I said she honestly doesn't know, it could be any one of the hundreds of black bus conductors in London. I think she had ridden with most of them.

SUNDAY, MAY 30TH

Last night went well for everyone and me. The theatre was about half full I think, I didn't really have enough confidence to look out at the seats, and because of the lights it was probably impossible to see anyway. After the show Bunty, who took three curtain calls, pointed out just one mistake when Charles came on stage a fraction to early while she was still showing off. Charles responded by telling her to 'fuck off sideways'. It was so funny to hear a posh bloke swear like me. Angela was still feeling lousy last night so she and Sally went back to the digs while the rest of us went for something to eat and to watch John and Gideon get pissed on barley wine. Bunty didn't come. She says that she has a dinner date with a producer who's just come back from Hollywood, which we all agreed was of course bollocks.

MONDAY, MAY 31ST

This morning while the rest of Liverpool were at work, I went to Sefton Park with Angela and Sally. We bought a dodgy hamburger from a stall in the park and sat on the grass for a while until it rained and ruined the whole day. Tonight's show was memorable for only one thing, Bunty taking yet another curtain call in front of an audience who had long since left the theatre and were on their way home.

TUESDAY, JUNE 1ST

I had unexpected early morning sex with Sally which was great but fraught with danger as Mrs Hughes was on the prowl. Once Sally had left I decided to go back to sleep but not before I remembered to feel how smug I am right now.

WEDNESDAY, JUNE 2ND

We had a very pissed-off Bunty on stage last night and it was brilliant to see. During the first Act in the bedroom scene as she was in full flow the audience suddenly burst into spontaneous applause drowning out her whining. She was furious and had the look of death on her face as she peered out into the stalls. Boxer and Liverpool hero John Conteh had arrived late with two glamour models and as they were being led to their seats the audience on seeing their hero responded by cheering and clapping like they were at a football match. As Bunty was fuming mid-speech on stage, Conteh began to wave thank you's to whoever cheered the loudest. At the end of Act One I thought Bunty was going to explode she was that red. Serves her right, she's horrible. After the show director John had three more extra barley wines than usual and celebrated by pissing in his trousers as they led him back to the Sandy Banks Hotel. Acting's a strange old business.

THURSDAY, JUNE 3RD

Scary Poppins had calmed down a bit tonight and the show went ok. Gideon is trying to convince everyone that John Conteh will be shot like President Kennedy in his next fight and that the bullet that kills him will have Bunty Swoon printed on it. Piss pants director John is back to normal and nobody has said a word about his soaked Tesco bomber jeans because we all like him.

FRIDAY, JUNE 4TH

The girls and me got a right telling off at breakfast this morning from Mrs Hughes about what she calls 'our fun and games at bedtime'. Her other guest Mr Ward is getting upset and she reminded us that she doesn't want him upset because he votes Conservative.

SATURDAY, JUNE 5TH

The whole cast minus Scary went to The Cavern today and we had a brilliant time. Groups were playing Beatles songs all day and the place was packed full. Charles was tasked with keeping John sober but it was a hopeless job and by three o'clock he was drunk again but trouser dry and able to stagger back to Sandy Banks for a sleep before the performance tonight. There was no knock on my door tonight so the warning from Mrs Hughes might have worked. Fucking Tories!

SUNDAY, JUNE 6TH

Rang Auntie Joan this morning and for once Amit didn't answer. In fact nobody did. I told Sally at breakfast and she said that perhaps Auntie Joan and Amit were still in bed. I never even thought of that. Oh God! The girls and me went to Sefton park and fed the ducks and later we met everyone minus Bunty of course, for Sunday lunch at a Berni Inn. The rumour around the table is that Bunty has moved into a posher hotel with the big nob from Hollywood. The rumour seems to have been started by Gideon so it's probably rubbish.

TUESDAY, JUNE 8TH

I made a stupid mistake in last night's performance but I got away with it because it got a big laugh and looked like it was all part of the play. David who plays the lawyer called for a drink to be brought to the drawing room by the errand boy (me). I walked on stage and stood beside him and then realised that I'd forgotten the bloody drink. I mumbled something like 'sorry sir, we're short of whisky', and quick as a flash David answered 'well it's a good job I'm a gin drinker then, now push off and fetch me one'. I didn't get told off by Scary Poppins and we are thinking of keeping it in tonight.

WEDNESDAY, JUNE 9TH

The audience was really small tonight. John reckons Liverpool have had enough of us and Somerset Maugham. I don't think we will be here next week, and the bedroom fun seems to have stopped as well. It was Gideon's birthday party tonight and we all went for a meal after the show but it was a very low key affair because Bunty and her new producer man turned up despite Gideon lying to them about where the party was. David says he wants to meet me by the bandstand in Sefton Park tomorrow lunchtime and I'm to bring the girls with me.

FRIDAY, JUNE 11TH

David is forming his own company to perform a pantomime at Christmas and he wants to recruit me, Gideon, Bette and the girls. Before we all go our separate ways on Sunday he wants my details. You have to sing and dance in pantomime though. It's the last night tomorrow night and I will be sorry to leave everyone. I wonder if the girls have got a special present for me. Liverpool looks like a really good place but it's just a bit too keen on football for me to like it too much.

SATURDAY, JUNE 12TH

I've woken up this morning with a terrible sore throat and a banging headache. I suppose it's a good thing that tonight's the last night. I stayed in bed most of today and felt sorry for myself but tonight the show must go on.

SUNDAY, JUNE 13TH

My head is banging again this morning but it's not a cold that's causing it. It seems sometime after the show in the pub I discovered that I like Bloody Marys. Angela is having breakfast without Sally who didn't come home last night. She was last seen kissing a Spanish boy called Juan who told her he played for Liverpool. Angela, sounding real jealous, said that he was only interested in having sex with Sally and was a dirty sod. I told her 'well it takes Juan to know Juan'. She didn't laugh.

TUESDAY, JUNE 15TH

Nobody will be surprised to know that I didn't get a big welcome when I came home on Sunday. In fact there was nobody in when I knocked on Auntie Joan's front door and I had to climb through the open toilet window to let myself in. Auntie Joan and Amit are sleeping in her bed at nights now, so I might have to leave. I went over to mum's yesterday and I got a lecture on being a Christian and how to be a shining example as she chain smoked Embassy number tens sitting on a tramp's lap. My family really are shit. Tomorrow morning I will go for a walk along the canal path and contemplate throwing myself in.

WEDNESDAY, JUNE 16TH

Something rather nice happened this morning. On my walk to the shops two young girls on their way to school said that they had seen me on the front of the *Jackie* mag. How good is that. Of course just when something good happens there's always something bad just around the corner. As I was coming out of Woolworth's after just buying Chirpy Chirpy Cheep Cheep (I know,) I bumped into Susan and her new boyfriend. His name's Brian and they were on their way to the car park where his Triumph Herald was parked. I have no right to feel bad about her being happy but I suppose I still like her a bit. Brian actually seemed quite a nice bloke for someone who drives a Triumph Herald. Lying in bed writing this I've decided that I must get away from Southall and rent a room somewhere in London to be near creative people like me, and not with two dirty old relatives, an ex-tramp, and an Indian gigolo and a bonkers ex-girlfriend.

FRIDAY, JUNE 18TH

A real boring day broken up by going out mid-afternoon to buy an *Evening News* and have a look at the flat share ads. I might have been a bit ambitious in thinking that I could afford something in London, but I have seen one in Ealing, which at least isn't in Southall. I have hardly seen any telly at all since I've been back and tonight the Black and White Minstrel Show was on again. It's not got any better or less insulting to anyone watching it.

SATURDAY, JUNE 19TH

It's Southall Carnival day so I got out of bed and had a look. Lots of good floats spoiled only by the sight of mum and Vince walking among them collecting for the orphans of a country I can't remember. How mum's changed. A few weeks ago those collection tins would have been emptied and spent on drink and dirty new uncles. The carnival queen is Anne Taylor who had the nickname of Marge at school because she laid down and spread easily, I'll bet the carnival organisers don't know that. I had a ninety nine for breakfast followed by cod and chips in the paper for dinner.

SUNDAY, JUNE 20TH

Nothing happening apart from the bloke on *The Golden Shot* trying to kill someone again, so I went to the pictures on my own of course. The Odeon was showing *Up Pompeii* the film from the telly programme. It wasn't very funny but did have some sexy girls in it and was better than *Dad's Army*.

MONDAY, JUNE 21ST

A bus ride to Greenford this morning to open a bank account. I was sent a cheque from Ace for thirty pounds so I needed to put it somewhere before I spent it being stupid like buying things such as Chirpy fucking Cheep Cheep. This afternoon I went to see the room in the flat at Ealing. A bloke called Guy answered the door and showed me around. The flat is small but my room seemed nice enough so I made a bit of a quick decision and said yes to the room. It is four pounds a week and

I buy my own Wimpy's and chocolate. Guy goes to Ealing Tech College and is an art student but he says his dad is loaded as he's a big knob at Esso. Guy seems ok. I'll move in on Saturday once I've told Auntie Joan.

TUESDAY, JUNE 22ND

Lucien rang this morning to say well done for doing good in Liverpool and he also said that Thames Television might want someone to play a black teenager in a new programme called *Love thy Neighbour*. He also said that it hasn't all been written yet but he would keep me in mind even though I wasn't 'completely black' whatever that means. He has though got me an audition for a Lilt advert next week, half a day's work, no dialogue just background, but it will pay a week's rent. I said thanks.

WEDNESDAY, JUNE 23RD

I need to get out soon. This Amit bloke is seriously getting on my tits. Who wants to hear your old white-haired auntie screaming out 'yes my Indian prince' at two o'clock in the morning?

THURSDAY, JUNE 24TH

Vince's mate Piggy Palmer has agreed to move me in his van on Saturday providing I give him three pounds petrol money. I said yes, but then reminded him that we're going to Ealing not fucking Scotland so he can have two pounds which is still a pound too much. I went out and got two boxes from the alley behind Woolworth's, and borrowed two of the new suitcases that mum stole from Daniels during her drinking days. Auntie Joan's sulking a bit I think but I don't know why. She only has eyes for Amit nowadays.

FRIDAY, JUNE 25TH

All packed up and ready to go at ten tomorrow providing Piggy Palmer turns up on time. I bought Auntie Joan a box of Milk Tray to say thank you for taking me in when Mum went funny. She seemed really happy when she opened them and she got up and gave me a cuddle. By the time she had sat down that fat, lazy, Amit had already eaten two strawberry creams and one of them barrel shaped ones.

SUNDAY, JUNE 27TH

I have finally moved in after yesterday's day of fun. Piggy Palmer turned up over an hour late in what can only be described as Coco the clown's spare car. It had only two windows and possibly less lights. Piggy wouldn't drive until I handed him the two pounds. I gave him one pound as a deposit and told him he could have the other one when and only when we arrived by some miracle in Ealing. An hour and a lot of swearing later we eventually arrived and I handed over the other pound and then went to knock up Guy. When I had finally woke him up I returned to find all my stuff dumped on the pavement and no sign of Piggy or the clown car. To be fair Guy came down in his Thunderbird pyjamas and helped me carry my stuff upstairs. I'm settled in now but will seek out Piggy Palmer for a refund when I go back and visit Auntie Joan.

MONDAY, JUNE 28TH

There's a brilliant little café downstairs on the high street where you can get two sausages, two eggs and chips for forty-five pence. I think I'm going to get really fat living here. I rang Lucien to tell him my change of address and phone number. The phone's downstairs in the corridor and it's a party line shared with the ladies' hairdressers next door. The Lilt ad is on Thursday. I should have the details tomorrow morning.

TUESDAY, JUNE 29TH

Guy plays the guitar in a group and they rehearse tonight in a room above the New Inn pub. I'm going along to watch. He seems dead impressed that I'm an actor, it's nice to be well thought of for once. There's been nothing in the post from Lucien today. Guy says that sometimes the post goes to the hairdressers by mistake. I'll ask in there tomorrow. I think Guy smokes dope, there was a funny smell coming from his room last night and I'm sure it wasn't from his bum.

WEDNESDAY, JUNE 30TH

Sure enough the details from Lucien were delivered to the hairdressers next door. Guy had warned me about the girls and he was right it didn't take them long to tease me. Theresa, the old girl who owns the hairdressers, reminds me of the old bags who were at the AEC although it seems that she doesn't like men very much. Guy says that she lives with a gardener called Lynn and has been a dyke all her life. There's a cute little blonde called Ginny who washes hair and also sweeps it up that I wouldn't mind having a bash at, but she looked at me like I had just trod in dog shit so I might not bother with her. I read the stuff about the Lilt ad in the café eating eggs, bacon and beans. Pretty soon I'll be so fat I'll have to buy my clothes from the fat bloke's catalogue that's in the doctors waiting room. The ad is being filmed in a warehouse in Wimbledon so at least I'm near an underground station now. Guy's rehearsal was cancelled last night when the room above the pub was double booked by a palm reader who runs a spiritualist meeting, somebody should have seen that coming.

THURSDAY, JULY 1ST

The Lilt ad was a big waste of time and train fare. I spent an hour on two trains and then another half an hour walking around trying to find the poxy warehouse only to be told when I finally got there that I was 'too white' for the filming. What the fuck does 'too white' mean? I was so fed up I seriously thought of chucking myself under a train on the way home, but I didn't because I realised that I had paid Guy a full month's rent.

FRIDAY, JULY 2ND

I'm going to a party tonight to meet Guy's friends from the college. I've searched out the Hai Karate and had a nice long bath while taking in the druggy smells that are coming from Guy's room.

MONDAY, JULY 5TH

Where the fuck did that weekend just go? The last two days have gone by and this morning I've had to ask Guy what happened. It seems in no particular order. I smoked pot sitting on the floor in a circle with everyone while listening to the Rolling Stones. I drank a whole Party four of beer and a bottle of Mateus Rose wine with my new best friend, a spot welder called Eric from Acton, and I spent at least eight hours in bed with a big girl called Dirty Mary who has had nine tenths of the local Ealing rugby club and most of their twenty-four supporters. I can't remember a thing about the drinking, drug taking or shagging, although I did wonder why I was wearing flares this morning that were two sizes too big for me. They must be Dirty Mary's. I won't smoke dope again.

TUESDAY, JULY 6TH

Back to Southall this morning to see mum and Vince at Auntie Joan's house. Why must my family always do things to embarrass me? I know that I've just spent a lost weekend with a lost woman and a lot of drugs, but at my age aren't I expected to do that? There is to be a double wedding in September when mum and Auntie Joan get hitched to Vince and Amit. I'm speechless. Old people should only be allowed to marry once otherwise it's just a big old waste of wedding cake and money. On the bus back home I remembered that mum hadn't actually been married yet, although it doesn't please me to remember that she's given men more relief than the St John's Ambulance service.

WEDNESDAY, JULY 7TH

I can't stop it, I was back on the dope today. Guy rolled a joint and was looking to share it with someone, I have very little willpower and it was easier to get stoned than cook something I suppose. Strangely, I thought of Sheila and her large bouncy tits and also Ringo Starr, as I drifted off to sleep in my drug-fuelled haze.

THURSDAY, JULY 8TH

Guy tells me this this morning that the two joints we smoked yesterday contained nothing more than old Holborn tobacco as he as out of marijuana. So how did I see Ringo having fun with Sheila and those breasts? I must be going bonkers. The phone in the corridor rang this afternoon. I was expecting a call from Lucien so I ran half naked down the stairs before the ringing stopped. I stubbed my toe on the bottom stair as I grabbed the receiver on what was possibly the last ring and answered. It was some old pensioner called Doris who wanted to book a shampoo and set from Theresa, bloody lesbian hairdressers.

FRIDAY, JULY 9TH

I rang Lucien myself today and by some miracle he said that he was just going to call me. What a coincidence! I have an audition for a Thames production called *Ace of Wands* on Monday, a children's programme filmed at Teddington. I'm to dress smartly and be prepared to read a piece from the first episode. My audition is at eleven, and I report to the reception desk. I'm definitely staying off the joints from now on, whether they contain marijuana or not. Guy says Dirty Mary is after me, I thought it was because she thinks I'm the best shag ever, but he says it's because she wants her flares back.

SATURDAY, JULY 10TH

Tonight in the Swan pub there is the double engagement party of you know who. I will go for ten minutes and leave, nobody will miss me. There were eleven people at the party, me, the four newly engaged, Amit's three teenage boys, two tramps called Harry and a do-gooder from the Sally Army called Trevor. Auntie Joan wasn't talking to Amit because he said she looked fat and was too old to wear a mini skirt. To be honest he was right. I had a half a lager shandy and then escaped through a window in the toilet cubicle, not the first time that I had done that. Mum will think that I'm a bad son for leaving without saying goodbye but then I think she's a bad mother, so we're even on that score.

SUNDAY, JULY 11TH

A nothing day although I did try and iron a shirt for tomorrow without much success. Guy's on the old Holborn next door again. Tonight he's definitely rehearsing with his group. The room above the pub is now available as the palm reader woman has suddenly been taken ill. Once again you'd have thought she should have seen that coming.

MONDAY, JULY 12TH

I've been to Teddington studios before *For the love of Ada* thing so I knew it would be an early start and lots of travelling. The audition was dead easy and I think I read well. I lied when the producer asked me if I liked science fiction. I said yes it was my best subject at school. When I was on the bus coming home I suddenly realised what a spanner I have been and what a stupid answer that was. Why the fuck didn't I say that I loved *Dr Who* or *Lost in Space*? Apart from being a twit I think they liked me and the stuff I had to act out with one of the production team seemed to go really well, but who knows? I'm getting a bit pissed off with Guy and him being stoned all the time, it's a bit scary and funny at the same time. I went to the laundrette tonight to get away for a bit and got chatted up by a large Jamaican woman called Pearl who wanted to cook me Jerk chicken and iron my Y-fronts. I said I'd think about and I'd let her know next Monday. She scared the shit out of me.

WEDNESDAY, JULY 14TH

Lucien rang and there's two jobs in the pipeline. A comedian called Stan Cutler is doing a summer season starting next week and his 'feed man has let him down by leaving'. He's looking for a quick replacement idiot. When Lucien got the call he said he immediately thought of me. Charming! If I did it that it would just leave me enough time to get back and do a couple of days filming on this *Ace of Wands* thing because they came back to Lucien and said I'd got the part. The *Idiot* part is in a place called Cromer in Norfolk and is for four weeks, the money's ok and I've got nothing else to do. The *Ace of Wands* thing seems a lot more exciting and is on telly peak time just when children are home from school and are eating their fishfingers and beans in front of the telly. So I'm off to Norfolk on Friday and old Stan is even paying my train fare. We do our first show on Monday afternoon.

THURSDAY, JULY 15TH

I told Guy this morning that I would be away for four weeks but he was busy stroking a lion who had slept in his bed all night while he had been playing Kerplunk with Clint Eastwood. He really does need to see a doctor about his drug taking. My bank account now says twenty eight pounds and I'm pretty happy about that, so happy in fact that I went to Millets and brought myself two shirts and a pair of Levi's. My train from Paddington station leaves at nine o' clock tomorrow so I will keep out of the way of Guy by having something to eat in the café and then going to the library to look up Cromer and travel to meet my new boss Stan.

SUNDAY, JULY 18TH

So I'm here and Stan's all right and seems a right good laugh for an old bloke who swears a lot and is capable of drinking twelve pints of beer in two hours. We have rehearsed today and are actually performing in a theatre at the end of a pier. Basically, this means that the theatre stands on something that looks like it might fall into the sea anytime a little gust of wind blows, possibly from Stan's beery arse. The first half of show Stan tells corny jokes while I occasionally bring on silly props, the most appropriate one being a kite because he suddenly develops noisy wind. At least the children in the audience might laugh. The second half though is quite good and will take some learning. We have to pretend to be decorators and put up wallpaper using some steps and buckets of wallpaper paste. Obviously things go wrong and we get covered in the paste and tear most of the paper while Stan skilfully falls off the steps. We've practised this twice now and it's hard but I'm enjoying it. I just hope people laugh tomorrow. We do two shows a day, one at two o'clock when Stan's sober and another one at seven o'clock when Stan's steaming drunk. The second show should be funnier. My digs are run by a husband and wife called Betty and Lou. I haven't yet worked out who is the male and who is the female. They both look like that comedy actress Peggy Mount.

MONDAY, JULY 19TH

Looking back through my notes in my books I realise that it's over a year now since I've left school. Lots have happened, some bad things but mostly good. I am an actor, I've been in adverts, toured in a play and been a pin up on the front cover of *Jackie*. Not bad for a half caste boy from Southall with no exam results. This afternoon I will be starting a summer season in Norfolk. I hope it goes well.

TUESDAY, JULY 20TH

Last night as Stan was sinking his tenth pint of the day, he said I was doing all right for starters. I'll take that as a compliment as

I thought I was awful. My timing was all off, and even though it got a big laugh from the children and some of their parents, I dropped a bucket of wall paper foam at the wrong time. Stan says to be mindful that the audience are on holiday and are in a good mood, so as long as we can make that good mood last until the next act when singer Frank Ifield gets on, then we've done our job. I think I've now worked out that Betty is definitely female because I caught Lou shaving in the bathroom this morning, although Peggy Mount looks like she could do with a swipe with a Wilkinson Sword whenever I've seen her on the telly.

WEDNESDAY, JULY 21ST

I don't know whether this is good or bad but Stan seems to be trusting me a lot more. He's going a bit higher up the steps confident that I will catch him when he does his comedy fall. So far it's all going to plan.

FRIDAY, JULY 23RD

Last night I was actually asked for my autograph as I left the theatre to go home, the person asking was only a ten-year-old girl but I wrote, To Julie, love Dessie x , with lots of pride and surprisingly very little embarrassment. When I got to the pub Stan was already on his third pint. I brought my Coke over to the table and told him about the autograph girl, but he didn't seem that impressed. Despite him being about a hundred years old and a drunkard, I actually quite like him.

SATURDAY, JULY 24TH

There's not a lot to do here but sleep and work. I found a café this morning that does egg sandwiches for fifteen pence so at least I can eat cheaply and save money. It belted down with rain all day so we were full. This fucking foamy paste mixture gets everywhere and the stage hands at the theatre are getting shirty with us. They have actually got to do some work now instead of drinking tea all day and popping next door to the amusement arcade to chat up the schoolgirls.

SUNDAY, JULY 25TH

Most of the dancers in the show look much too old for me but there seems to be one that is interested in me. I've got a problem however because the dancer in question is called Graham and the bugger won't stop looking at me.

MONDAY, JULY 26TH

Stan accidentally dropped a paste brush on my head tonight and it hurt so much that I shouted out 'fuck' as it dropped to the ground. The mic above the stage picked it up and all the children in the audience now have a new word to practise. In the pub later I thought I'd better apologise to Stan but on reflection I think he was so pissed from the afternoon session today I don't think he even noticed me swearing or him dropping the brush.

TUESDAY, JULY 27TH

So there has been three complaints today from the parents of children who said fuck as they were being put to bed last night. I don't believe a word of it, those lazy stagehands were pissing themselves with laughter as the stage manager bollocked us this afternoon. In the pub Stan told me that it's important to stay focused and professional, as he sank his fifth pint of the afternoon before tonight's performance.

WEDNESDAY, JULY 28TH

Graham told me today that he hopes to move to London soon as he has an audition for the Young Generation when the season ends. I told him that I might be moving to Glasgow when the season ends.

SUNDAY, AUGUST 1ST

Something terrible has happened. Stan's dead. On Thursday night as we were going down a storm on stage, the poor old sod literally fell down the ladder backwards as he was having a massive heart attack. I stood and watched as he actually died on stage, not realising what had just happened the audience laughed at the way he fell so hilariously. The curtain closed as I started to cry, I just knew he had croaked. An ambulance rushed Stan to hospital and a police car took me to the police station. A horrible person called Sergeant Bastard (not his real name) questioned me for about an hour on what had happened, I don't know why, there must have been five hundred people who saw what went on. I got back to the digs at one in the morning to find the front door locked and nobody around so I sat on a bench on the pier all night watching two seagulls kissing as the sun came up. The police told me yesterday that Stan has a wife called Pam who lives in Huddersfield and she would like to talk to me as I was the last person to see him alive. I never even knew that he was married, he didn't tell me. Tomorrow I will go to Huddersfield. For the past two weeks Stan made me and a lot of people very happy, going to see Pam is the least I can do.

Now, where's Huddersfield?